JIGGLEBOX

It's the journey not the end

RICK MCKINNEY

To you who fight to be yourself

Well I'm going to New York City, and I'm leaving on a train, if you want to stay behind and wait til I get back again, today's gray skies, tomorrow is tears, you'll have to wait til yesterday is here. If you wanna go where the rainbows end, you'll have to say goodbye. All our dreams come true baby, up ahead, and it's out where your memories lie. Well the road is out before me, the moon is shining bright. What I want you to remember as I disappear tonight, today's gray skies, tomorrow is tears, you'll have to wait til yesterday is here.

TOM WAITS

THE END

Scavengers picking through the ashes. Children of the mills, children of the junkyards. Sleepy, illiterate, fuzzy little rats. Haunted, paint-sniffin' stoned out of their shaved heads, forgotten, foraging, mystical children, foul-mouthed, glassy eyed, hallucinating...

PATTI SMITH

Once upon a time, it was 1998. The Norman Rockwell portrait of the Great American Dream had withered and cracked. But Mr. & Mrs. Dorian Grey, Anytown, USA had yet to get the message. For America, the wakeup call, the beginning of the end, was a few years away. For our hero, the day was today. Maybe.

Salem Schofield sat on a motel bed, loading rounds into the clip of a 9mm Spanish military pistol. Curtains hung crookedly on a bent rod, their floral pattern faded to a smear under years of grime. The air was stale, thick with the faint tang of cigarette smoke and despair. Spread across the bed were several steno notebooks, the covers scribbled with bits of poetry and glued-on magazine imagery.

Salem was in his mid-thirties, a tad overweight and lined of face. Once a handsome man, his features had grown hard, timeworn. His eyes were anxious, his jaw tense with an unspeakable and endless ache. Long, dirty-blonde hair with a seaweed green tint hung limp on the shoulders of his ragged brown corduroy jacket. The pale green in his hair looked less like a deliberate choice and more like the residue of time that it was. Moss on an old, abandoned car in the woods. His corduroy jacket, worn to a near-sheen in places, smelled faintly of damp earth.

The TV was on. An old western was playing. A gunfight broke out. Salem's hands moved methodically, detached, performing a ritual he had rehearsed a hundred times. It occurred to Salem that the 9mm might have been the only gun ever purchased with poetry.

"Yeah, I did that," he mumbled, remembering having traded ad space in his poetry quarterly *ZipZap* for the gun. "And yet here we sit. Yup, I'm a nobody." Then, in an imitation Brando voice, "I coulda been a contender."

On the TV, cowboys exchanged gunfire in a dusty town square, their movements exaggerated, theatrical. The chaos of the scene stood in contrast to the still life of the room. Salem lifted the remote, and the crack of revolvers suddenly thundered as he turned the volume all the way up. He fit the clip into the gun, hammered it home with the butt of his left hand, sat back against the headboard of the bed, lifted the gun to his temple, and closed his eyes.

Behind his eyelids, he saw a blue sky, leafless winter trees, cigarette smoke billowing in slow motion past a cigarette-holding feminine hand. Over the howl of a locomotive engine, an engineer's voice whispered in horror, "No," followed by a slamming sound that would ring in his ears for eternity, he figured. The locomotive's brakes screamed. The wheels of the locomotive seized and ground metal to metal, throwing sparks.

Blood splattered an embankment of fresh winter snow.

Back in the motel, Salem's eyes snapped open, startled by the vision. He stared at the TV, taking a few deep breaths, then slid back the hammer to cock the gun. He closed his eyes and winced. The gunfight ended and suddenly, annoyingly, a commercial came on advertising a new housing development. Salem opened one eye, then the other, his expression shifting from anticipated pain to disgust. He lowered the gun shook his head and, without hesitation fired at the TV set. The TV's vacuum tube imploded in a puff of smoke.

The ignominious demise of the hapless television filled the room with shards of glass and the acrid stench of burnt plastic. Smoke curled from the shattered remains, the once-cheerful commercial now reduced to silence. Salem exhaled slowly, his breath trembling as the echo of the gunshot faded.

✳ ✳ ✳

Salem opened the accordion door of a phone booth and stepped inside. Turning, he fought with the door, lifted the receiver, and dialed 1-800-USA-RAIL. Fits of melancholia often triggered an impulse in Salem to dial 1-800-USA-RAIL. Amtrak let you make reservations free of charge, and the reservation agents were mostly women. He found their feminine voices soothing, and the agents seemed to share in the magic of coloring in the black and white lines of future train travel itineraries. Though he rarely took the trips he planned with them, just making a plan afforded him tremendous comfort, an escape from his impoverished and pain-addled existence.

This time, however, Salem felt himself to be far beyond mere melancholy and on a mission to finish out the tragic comedy of his life. This trip he would take.

"Yes, I'd like to book a reservation for the soonest possible departure. Where to? Anywhere. As far as I can go in one shot. Departure city? Seattle." His voice carried the weary sarcasm of someone who had long since stopped expecting anything from the world.

"What? Christmas? No, I'm not going home for the holidays. If I had a home, would I be asking you to send me just anywhere? Look, just…"

He rolled his eyes as he waited.

"Boston, huh?"

Salem paused to think.

"Let's make it Connecticut. Killingsworth, Connecticut. What? You don't go through there anymore?" Salem's fingers tightened around the receiver. *The fucking American rail system,* he thought to himself. He had spent a year in Germany in his youth. The rail map of the United States was a joke to Europeans. Put on hold by the customer service agent, Salem drifted into his mind.

A passenger train sat stopped in the woods. The forest maintained a funeral silence but for the staccato incantations of police radios and the crunch of boots in the snow. Amtrak policemen slowly walked the tracks. Like children in a war zone, they hopscotched over things unnatural as they went.

Salem stood wrapped in a gray wool blanket. A kind of death shroud worn in sympathy, it revealed only his nose and mouth. From the darkness above his nose, he stared down at a kidney-shaped patch of bloodstained snow. Somewhere in the back of his mind, a voice said it *IS* a kidney. Denial. Mental image of a door slamming shut. In the traumatized mind, one door closes so that others may open.

Now, sirens cried in the distance. Salem's exhalations hung suspended in the frozen forest air like empty voice bubbles in an unfinished cartoon. The steam rising from the locomotive was likewise mute. Machine empathy. No clear dialogue could be heard. Only mumbles and radio static.

A voice on a payphone in a time warp snapped him back.

"Huh? Old Saybrook? Never heard of it. Ten miles away? Sounds fine."

THE JOURNEY

We sail tonight for Singapore. We're all as mad as hatters here. I've fallen for a tawny moor. Took off to the land of nod. Drank with all the Chinamen. Walked the sewers of Paris. I danced along a colored wind. Dangled from a rope of sand. You must say goodbye to me.

TOM WAITS

Salem sat slumped in a coach seat in sunglasses and ragged brown corduroy jacket. A steno notebook lay open in his lap, a Pentel Rolling Writer pen poised in his hand. At his feet were a small backpack and a narrow white box containing a 5-liter bladder of wine. The clickety-clack of the train wheels announcing the spaces between tracks formed a constant background of hypnotic percussion.

His faded seaweed-green hair fell across his face. He blew it away, but it fell back again. He repeated this absentmindedly. Outside, the night was pitch black, but the train barreled forward at full speed. Clickety-clack clickety-clack clickety-clack.

Salem reached into his jacket, pulled out a prescription bottle, and poured its contents into his palm. A colorful array of pills of various shapes and sizes revealed themselves under the dim overhead lights.

Plucking two yellow pills, Salem popped them into his mouth and returned the rest to the bottle, the bottle to his jacket pocket. He resumed his slumped position. The train vibrated and sang through the night.

In the fairy tale, if you choose to grow up, you can't come back to Never Never Land. For some, however, the fairy tale works differently. You grow up, but Never Never Land never lets you go. Salem had done much of his growing up on trains. Perhaps for that reason, the train and Never Never Land had, for him, become one and the same.

Salem leaned his head back, closed his eyes, and rocked to sleep. In sleep he dreamed.

✳ ✳ ✳

In dream time, in quantum time where all realities exist simultaneously, an 11-year-old Salem with white-blond hair, bright eyes and maroon plaid bell bottom pants sat in a high-backed rocking chair in a suburban living room. He frowned as he stared out a large picture window. On the back swing, his feet dangled above the burnt orange shag carpeted floor. Outside, the sky was bruised black and purple. The boy's expression brightened momentarily when a flash of lightning streaked across the horizon. Across from him, his mustachioed salesman father sat on the edge of a faded armchair, leaning forward with his elbows on his knees. He was nervous, struggling to find the right words.

"You see, son, sometimes mommies and daddies have to go live in different houses so that they can, um, be happy again. Uh, for themselves." His voice was gentle, deliberate. "Mommy and Daddy have a special love for you that will never go away, no matter what. But sadly, the love between mommies and daddies isn't always forever."

A low rumble of thunder followed his words, and young Salem's eyes lit up again, his smile returning as rain began to pour outside.

"Son? Do you understand what I'm saying?" his father asked, but the boy abstained. His gaze remained fixed on the storm, grasping at its beauty, practically crawling out of his skin and through the picture window to escape the impact of the words he was hearing.

Later on a train platform, Salem stood transfixed as a wizard-ling man with long yellow beard tobacco stained around his mouth bent copper wire into the shape of an old steam engine. The artist's hands moved deftly, and young Salem's face lit up as the train took form.

Nearby, his mother sat smoking on a bench, her eyes scanning the tracks. She watched Salem distractedly always glancing down the line, looking for the incoming train.

"Salem! Get back here," she called, waving him over. "Your father's train is almost here."

Salem dragged his feet, returning to her side at a snail's pace.

His mother leaned in close, her voice suddenly urgent. "Now, honey, listen to Mommy. This is very important. You know how much I love you, and because I love you, I know what's best for you. Your father put this idea in your head—I know he did—so I don't blame you, okay? But listen to me very carefully."

The train screeched into the station, the noise almost drowning out her words. She grabbed Salem's jaw, pulling his face close to hers as his white hair danced in the blast of wind.

"Salem? If you decide to go and live with your father, that's it. There's no coming home again."

She yelled to be heard over the roar of the locomotive. Salem stared at her, wide-eyed.

❊ ❊ ❊

Now on the commuter train, young Salem sat across from his father. The man stroked his mustache nervously, glancing at his son, who sat on his hands, his legs crossed, swinging his feet. Salem stared out the window, watching clouds drift lazily across the sky.

"She said that?" his father asked, his voice low and uncertain. "She *actually* said that?"

Salem lowered his head and nodded silently.

After a pause, his father sighed heavily. "Salem, your mother is a very sick woman."

Salem didn't react. His gaze remained fixed on the clouds outside, his mind drifting far from the present. The shapes in the sky morphed before his eyes—white islands floating in an endless blue ocean. Between them, a majestic Spanish galleon sailed, its sails billowing in the wind of his imagination.

The boy smiled faintly at the vision. His father bit his lower lip, struggling to keep his emotions in check. He closed his eyes and shook his head.

❊ ❊ ❊

A 13-year-old Salem now sat alone in a coach seat of a cross-continental train. In the two years since his parents' divorce, he had grown taller, his delicate features taking on a striking, almost ethereal quality. His fair complexion and long lashes lent him an androgynous beauty.

A young conductor in his early twenties stopped to collect Salem's ticket. The man's face appeared friendly and open, with round, soft features and straight brown hair.

"Traveling all by yourself, little buddy?" the conductor asked with a smile.

"Yes, sir," Salem replied, his voice polite but guarded.

"Well now, if there's anything I can do for you, you just holler for Johnny, okay?"

Salem nodded. The conductor moved on, opening the door to the next car. Once Salem looked away, Johnny paused and glanced back, watching the boy for a moment longer before continuing on his route.

Later that night, in the lower level of the train, a toilet flushed. Salem emerged from the bathroom stall, his movements sluggish with exhaustion. He started toward the staircase leading back to his seat when Johnny stepped out from a nearby sleeper room.

"Hey there, little buddy," Johnny whispered. "Getting any sleep up there in those coach seats?"

Salem rubbed his eyes and shook his head.

Johnny winked. "Come here," he said in a conspiratorial tone. "Now, I'm not supposed to do this, 'cause, ya know, ya gotta pay big bucks for a sleeper on the train. But, um, you look like a nice kid, and I got an extra bunk, so... oh, I dunno. You're not gonna rob me or anything, are ya, kid?"

"No, sir!" Salem replied quickly, eager to accept the offer.

"Well, all right then! Come on in," Johnny said, waving him over.

Inside the dimly lit sleeper room, Salem lay in the lower bunk, his hands folded awkwardly over his stomach as Johnny talked. Johnny peered down from the top bunk, his face partially illuminated by the faint moonlight streaming through the window.

"Really? You've never had a wet dream?" Johnny asked, his voice casual but curious.

Salem frowned slightly. "I... I don't know. Maybe."

"Well, if you had, you'd know it," Johnny said with a chuckle. "It's the best thing ever."

"Really? I dunno," Salem replied hesitantly. "It sounds kinda strange."

Johnny grinned. "I could show you how."

Salem stiffened, his voice faltering. "Um, that's okay, really. I think maybe I should sleep."

"Okay," Johnny said with a shrug. "But don't blame old Johnny when your friends make fun of you 'cause they've all been doing it for years, and you're the last one."

Salem shifted uncomfortably, his exhaustion evident in his glassy eyes. After a long pause, he exhaled shakily and mumbled, "Okay, Johnny."

Johnny climbed down from his bunk and slid into bed beside Salem. A long silence ensued.

Steady moonlight and the occasional flickering light of a passing streetlamp illuminated the blanket beneath which Johnny's hand moved in time to the clickety clack song and sway of the train.

Salem's eyes opened and closed as he struggled to stay awake. "Are you sure this is right, Johnny?" he mumbled. "It feels strange."

"It's gonna be great. It's gonna feel really good, you'll see."

The train moved fast through the moonlit night as Salem succumbed to sleep.

How much time had elapsed Salem couldn't say when Johnny jostled him awake, getting him on his feet. Johnny peered left and right down the hall and then shuffled the sleepwalking Salem to the toilet.

The light in the bathroom was bright and garish, and Salem shielded his eyes as Johnny led him to the toilet.

"I don't what the matter is don't know why this ain't working." Johnny said with a frown.

"I'm... sorry," Salem replied, his head down.

"Maybe you're broken."

✳ ✳ ✳

A few years later Salem sat in the back of a tour bus trying to focus. His eyes wouldn't cooperate. Right out of high school, he had taken a job as a roadie for a band for their summer tour. The tour manager, Helen, a woman a decade his senior, was his boss. She had been hitting on him for weeks and not at all subtly. Salem got a lot of welcomed attention from young girls on the tour, and it made him feel bad that he couldn't return Helen's affections. He couldn't recall having ever learned that his body was his own and that he needn't feel guilty for not wanting to share it with anyone interested. Despite his protestations and making it very clear he didn't share her attraction for him, her advances had continued unabated and escalated into physical grabs and pinches.

Helen now sat beside him rubbing her hair against his cheek as he wondered how he'd come to be alone with her in the back of the bus. *Where is everyone?* He wondered. *And why won't my eyes focus?* He realized that his body didn't share his willingness to move.

Unbeknownst to Salem, his boss had laced his drink with Rohypnol, a benzodiazepine frequently used to forcibly knock people out and or take advantage of them while they can't fight back. For most people, the dosage she slipped him would have spelled a total blackout. No memory of the incident. But Salem had practically cut his teeth on heavy prescription drugs. When he was just 14 his mother had given him the narcotic butalbital for a migraine. A barbiturate brand named Fiorinal, it was just what doctors commonly prescribed for migraines at the time. As Salem's struggles with chronic headaches continued to grow, so too did his body's tolerance of narcotics. Ergo, although his boss didn't know it, she had doped a pill junkie and therefore only half effectively.

Helen pulled off Salem's pants and mounted him. Although he didn't remember much, he remembered enough. Later, when he reported to Helen's boss what any woman would clearly call rape, the much older man laughed at him.

"Yeah, like you could get it up on roofies!" the man said, looking away. Looking back at Salem out of the corner of an eye, he asked, "What do you want from me, kid?"

Salem realized he didn't know what he wanted aside from acknowledgement. He admitted that his memory was spotty like a half empty slide carousel but that which he could remember was very clear. He couldn't move his arms, he said, but he had performed. He was sure of that. The man just laughed more saying there was no way, that men couldn't be raped. Surely Salem had wanted it.

"She's hot," his boss said. "Consider yourself lucky, kid. I'd do her in a heartbeat."

As Salem left his office, the man shouted after him. "Hey, like I said it's not, you know, even physically possible. But I won't say anything if you don't. Sure would be an embarrassment for you, for her too but mostly for you if it got out."

❊ ❊ ❊

Students came and went from an ivy-laced entryway of a university building, books under their arms. A sign on a door of the English Department building read: *Office of the Dean of Letters.*

It was a few years later. A 21-year-old Salem sat across a large oak desk from the Dean. At this time of his life, Salem had spiked bleach-blonde hair, an earring, and round, red-rimmed glasses.

"You want to do your thesis on *what*?" the Dean asked, incredulous.

"Train travel. Yes, sir."

"No."

"But sir, the romance of train travel," Salem stuttered. "It's what I love. I love writing first and foremost, so what better way to foster that love and talent than by writing on a subject that fascinates me? Isn't that your job? To encourage us to succeed at what we love?"

"No and no again," the Dean replied. "Two reasons. One, our goal is to produce published writers, and no one would want to read a book about U.S. train travel. What does Amtrak have left now, four cross country routes? Three? I'm bored already. And two, I'm giving it to you straight, Schofield. You're a lousy writer. You have no concept of character or structure. And you use the first person pronoun like the whole world depends on what you think, which they don't. And they won't. Ever. I suggest you pursue a career in journalism—they're a lot looser over there. Either that or mortuary science, because you're killing me. Now go smoke dope or whatever you nonconformist types do nowadays. You're dismissed."

❉ ❉ ❉

Back in the world of the present on Amtrak, the train raced through the night, the rhythmic hum of the wheels on the tracks blending with the soft snoring of passengers in the coach car.

Across the aisle from Salem, an elderly couple swayed gently with the motion of the train. The woman's head rested on the man's shoulder, her silver hair catching the faint glow of the overhead lights.

Salem sat slumped in his seat, his green-tinted hair falling into his eyes. Beside him sat Agnes, a lumberjack-sized buxom woman with auburn hair and strikingly beautiful features. Her blue jean overalls looked as though they'd seen a lifetime of wear but they contrasted perfectly with the frilly white blouse she wore beneath. Her eyes sparkled with good humor.

"And that was that," Salem said, finishing his story.

"What did you do then?" Agnes asked, leaning in with genuine curiosity.

Salem smiled faintly, a wry expression crossing his face. "I went behind his back and published a small run of the book through the university. I knew he was pissed because he did everything he could to bust me for using school computers and shit. I graduated a year later, and you know what? Neither he nor any of my other professors ever congratulated me or recognized my achievement."

"Those fuckers!" Agnes exclaimed.

"Yeah," Salem agreed, his voice soft with lingering disappointment.

"So, can I buy the book somewhere? What's the title?" she asked, her tone hopeful.

"No. It was never published commercially. Drag, huh? I lost the courage, whatever. I tried, but I couldn't take the rejection. I got a lot of rejection. Nobody liked the title, for starters."

"What was it called?"

"Jigglebox, after a poem I wrote about a particularly jiggly train between Chicago and New York. I thought it was gonna vibrate right off the tracks and into a worm hole."

"What's your passion, Agnes?" Salem asked, his tone shifting to curiosity.

"What's my passion? My passion?! Wow, I think that's the first time anyone's asked me that." She paused, as if testing the words. "My job—now I get that all the time. I'm a trainer for sled dogs."

"No way. That's your job?"

"That's my passion," Agnes corrected, smiling warmly. "I've got a whole sled team. Beautiful creatures."

"Wow. That's very cool. I won't even ask what you do for work, cuz I can tell you'd rather not talk about it." Salem leaned back, a glimmer of life returning to his voice. "You wanna hear one of my train travel stories?"

"Yeah!" Agnes said enthusiastically.

"Cool." Salem sat up straighter.

"I was in Switzerland at the time. I'd been traveling on trains for months and was finally at the end of my savings. Although savings is an absurd term given that I have always lived right on the razor's edge, on *starvings* rather than savings having never had enough of anything to save. I had to get to Portugal, where an old friend's family owned a place on the coast and had invited me to stay out the summer promising me food wine surf and topless Dutch beauties. But first, I planned on seeing a friend from Hollywood who was staying in Madrid."

Gesticulating wildly as he got into his tale, Salem hypnotically transported Agnes and himself to faraway Europe...

A younger Salem, his hair tied back with a red bandana and an old army backpack slung over his shoulder, stood in a spotless Swiss train station. He carefully counted out massive weighty Swiss coins and rainbow-colored currency at the ticket counter, sliding them across to the clerk. With nothing more than a brief nod of his head, the clerk handed him a ticket. One single ticket.

Salem glanced at the ticket in his hand, reading the destination printed in bold letters. *That's it?* He wondered. In his naive estimation, he envisioned one train zipping along southward all the way to his destination.

Over the following days, however, he moved from train to train— a German train, then a French one, then a Spanish train, then a Portuguese train, the landscape changing subtly with each leg of the trip.

The changes in the landscape might have been subtle but the

changes in the quality and the speed of trains were dramatic. The Swiss train full of shining chrome, soft lighting and plush carpet whispered along seemingly seamless tracks at frightening speed with almost no one aboard. It was hushed like a library and clean as a commercial kitchen before inspection. Then came the train across France and into Spain from Geneva. This was a step down in class and comfort. A little less hushed and not quite so fast. Not quite so shiny and new. Then came a Spanish train, slower still and more populated and noisier and dirty.

In time Salem found himself crushed into a dark subway car in Madrid. The train, jam packed with commuters, jolted and swayed erratically. The lights overhead flickered on and off and dimmed, an erratic electrical connection from the train rocking, the wheels constantly losing contact with the power rail.

He laughed at his initial vision of one train all the way to the Mediterranean. He wondered how it all worked, how the Swiss rail company could sell him one ticket that somehow communicated all these changes of trains and now a subway, and all this before a united Europe. Before he reached his destination there would be more trains and a bus and even a boat to take him from one side of Lisbon to the other. The final train across a deserted stretch of Portugal would roll about as slowly as the Swiss train had gone fast. There would be no central air, only open windows and doors on an ancient train crawling at a horse's trot with chickens roosting in the luggage racks and old women dressed all in black and a gaping hole beneath the toilet large enough to fall through or shove a chicken through. And boy would it be hot.

At a payphone in the bustling Madrid train station, Salem dialed a number he had carefully written down on a scrap of paper. He held the phone tightly to his ear, his face brightening when the line connected.

"Joey? It's Salem! Oh, thank God. I made it to Madrid! I'm here!"

The excitement in his voice faltered as Joey's response came through the line. Salem's expression shifted to confusion, then disappointment.

"Huh? What do you mean *am I already here*? You've been inviting me for months. What's that? You have houseguests? Call you from my hotel? Uh-huh. In a few days. Okay. Sure, Joey. Yeah, we'll have lunch. See ya."

He hung up the phone slowly, his hand lingering on the receiver. His gaze drifted to a Spanish woman standing nearby.

"That was my buddy Joey. He's from Hollywood." Salem's voice was dry, edged with sarcasm. "He wants to *do lunch*. Can you beat that? Do lunch!! The guy knows perfectly well I'm broke and five thousand miles from home. So why did he invite me? Fuckin Hollywood people."

The Spanish woman watched him, her expression shifting from surprise to confusion to amusement as he spoke. A small smile crept across her face.

"Hoolly-woot!" she repeated, her accent thick but warm.

On the Madrid train platform, Salem stood beneath a sign displaying the words *Surcharge: 20 Pesetas.* The phrase was translated beneath it in several languages, but the meaning was the same: he didn't have enough money.

He opened his palm, revealing a handful of small coins, and shook his head. His gaze darted to the train waiting at the platform. Panic flickered across his face as the conductor's whistle blew.

The train was overcrowded, its aisles filled with people sitting on backpacks or standing shoulder-to-shoulder. The air was thick with the scent of sweat and the murmur of conversations in a dozen different languages, none of them English.

Salem squeezed into a corner near the back of the car, his backpack tucked beneath him as he sat on the floor. The sun dipped below the horizon, casting the train in dim shadows as it pulled away from Madrid.

Through the narrow aisle behind a sea of faces, Salem watched the conductor moving slowly but steadily through the crowd, collecting tickets and the surcharge. Each time the conductor took a step closer, Salem's anxiety grew. He leaned his head back against the wall, closing his eyes tightly as though willing himself to be invisible. Outside the train crawled along at the pace of a man walking.

In no time the conductor was only a few feet away but fortunately still a few people deep. Salem opened his eyes and glanced toward the open door. The train that had been moving at a crawl for the last hour was now, miraculously, at a dead stop.

Grabbing his backpack, Salem made his move. Catlike he do-si-do'd passed a few people stuck like him standing in the space between cars and stepped gingerly out of the train and onto the tracks. His heartbeat thundered in his ears. Salem walked quickly along the side of the train, moving in the opposite direction of the conductor. The night air was cool and filled with the faint hum of insects.

"Mitt Gottes hilfe" he whispered under his breath in his now near-fluent conversational German. His feet crunched softly on the gravel. Two cars ahead, he spotted an open door and climbed back inside just as the train jolted to life again. The car was slightly less crowded, perhaps only three to a seat instead of four, with only a handful of passengers huddling near the entrance. A couple of them smiled knowingly and nodded at him as he stood catching his breath. Salem returned the smile, sheepish but relieved.

Salem slumped down onto his backpack and gave in to exhaustion. *How long has it been since Zurich? A day? Two days?* He wondered. He had hardly slept. Was he asleep when it happened? Hard to say. He sat upright, his head nodding forward and then lolling to the side as the train swayed gently on the tracks. Now a hand reached into view, lightly tapping Salem on the cheek. The fabric of the sleeve was unmistakable—a conductor's uniform.

Salem's eyes flew open. Standing over him, the Spanish conductor stared down with a disapproving frown. "Has pagado el impuesto?"

Salem blinked, uncomprehending, as panic welled in his chest. Before he could stammer a response, a man sitting across from him spoke up in fluent Spanish.

"Sí, él lo pagó."

The conductor's expression softened slightly, though his skepticism lingered. He hesitated for a moment before nodding curtly and moving on.

Wide-eyed and shaken, Salem turned to the man who had spoken on his behalf. "What did you say to him?"

The man shrugged casually, a small smile playing on his lips. "I told him you paid."

Salem stared wide-eyed at the stranger for a long moment then nodded, mouthed the words thank you, dropped his head and fell back into an exhausted slumber.

❊ ❊ ❊

Back in the here and now on Amtrak somewhere in the United States the next morning, sunlight streamed through the train's windows, casting long beams of gold across the seats. Salem stirred, the warm light tugging him out of sleep. Slowly, he sat up, rubbing his eyes.

His notebook was still in his lap, one hand resting on it while the other clutched his sunglasses. He stretched, wincing at the stiffness in his neck, and turned to the seat beside him. Agnes was gone. He lingered for a moment, staring at the empty space. There was the smell of balony in the air. Someone's lunch from home. Resigned, he sighed and turned toward the window.

The train was passing through a small American town. The tracks ran parallel to the main avenue, where a parade of corporate logos flashed by: Wal-Mart, Taco Bell, Blockbuster Video, Motel 6,

Subway. Each sign felt like a reminder of something Salem didn't want to think about.

Reaching into his jacket, he pulled out the prescription bottle again, letting two yellow pills fall into his palm. He swallowed them dry, slipping the bottle back into his pocket.

Next, he fished a pair of headphones from his breast pocket and fitted them over his ears. After fumbling briefly with his portable CD player, he pressed play.

The raw, gravelly voice of Tom Waits filled his ears, accompanied by a haunting piano melody:

"I just want you to be happy, that's my only little wish..."

Leaning back in his seat, Salem flipped open his notebook. His pen moved quickly, scrawling the words "FUCK HAPPY!" across the top of a fresh page in bold, angry letters.

The music in Salem's headphones continued, Tom Waits' gravelly voice weaving a melancholy backdrop as Salem stared down at his notebook. His pen hovered for a moment before he began scribbling furiously, filling the page with fragmented thoughts, abstract lines of poetry, and looping doodles.

In his mind, his father's voice mingled with Waits' lyrics, distorting into a bitter refrain: *"I just want you to be happy... I just want you...*

"TO GET A JOB!" Salem shouted aloud, suddenly all eyes on him in the surrounding seats. Salem smiled and shrugged his shoulders in a non-verbal expression of oops. Mildly embarrassed but suddenly aware of the time-space shifting and pain-softening magic action of the pills, Salem closed his eyes and drifted back in time.

* * *

A younger Salem sat in the waiting room of a local newspaper office, a bold printed sign on the wall reading: *The Daily Herald: Award-winning journalism since 1925.* Another sign said, *A Gannett Corporation Company.* His knee bounced nervously as he glanced at a clipboard in his lap.

Later, Salem filled out a job application at a different office. As he flipped to the second page, the words *We drug test* were stamped in bold red letters at the top. His lips tightened into a thin line. A moment later, he set the clipboard down and walked out.

Now Salem was waiting tables in a crowded restaurant. Balancing a tray of coffee cups, he tripped, the liquid spilling all over a customer. The man leapt to his feet, his face twisted in anger, and threw Salem a gut punch, knocking the wind out of him.

Now Salem stood loading packages onto a UPS truck in obvious haste. His breath was visible, and sweat dripped down his temples as he heaved heavy boxes in the cold of a warehouse. A supervisor in a warm brown coat with a hood stood nearby, stopwatch in hand, shaking his head in disapproval. An hour later, Salem slumped into a folding chair during a brief break, his body sagging with exhaustion. The same supervisor poked his head around a corner and pointed at his wristwatch in the noisy distribution hub indicating breaks over.

Now it was the late 1980s and a wildly painted, toy-encrusted boxy early model American car pulled into the driveway of a beige three-bedroom ticky-tacky suburban family clone home, indistinguishable from a thousand of its neighbors. The car, adorned with deer antlers, baby doll body parts, electronic circuit boards, neon-haired trolls, and thousands of army men, farm animals, dinosaurs and other smaller figurines, stood out starkly in the otherwise uniform suburban development.

Salem stepped out of the car, his blue-dyed hair sticking out in every direction. He smiled at his vehicle before heading inside.

Inside the house, everything was white or beige—glass tabletops, faux Grecian urns, woven baskets, and similar decor. The home had been one of four initial design models used to sell the whole subdivision. In the living room and entry area it appeared his mother had simply moved in amidst the generic model decor.

"Yo, Mom? You here? Anybody home?" Salem's voice echoed through the museum like space.

A phone rang in another room. Salem rushed to the kitchen and grabbed the phone hanging on the wall.

"Oh, hi Dad. Yeah, I'm all right. No. Dad, I quit that sucky job weeks ago. I had to kiss yuppie ass all day long, Dad. Yeah, I've interviewed elsewhere. No, it wasn't my hair. Everybody wants to piss test, Dad. No, I don't smoke pot, I just think it's dead wrong to go prying into someone's piss. It's an invasion of privacy."

As he spoke, Salem picked up a pile of opened mail on the kitchen table, sorting through it. He pulled out one letter addressed to his mother. Boldly scrawled across the address label in his mother's handwriting were the words: "Salem's problem."

"No, whoa, whoa, hold it. Dad, I gotta job. I'm a writer, remember? No, I can't write in my spare time, it just doesn't work like that. Look, I gotta go. Yeah, you too. Bye."

Ending the call, Salem opened the letter. The header read: Serenity Village Homeowners Association. He scanned the text, shook his head, and began reciting it aloud in an authoritative voice with a dose of sarcasm.

"Recently the Homeowners Association has received numerous complaints regarding an 'eye-sore' in the neighborhood. These complaints concern your 'graffiti car.' While the Association appreciates your individuality and freedom of expression, we suggest you consult your Association Rules and Regulations where you will see that such a violation of neighborhood aesthetics is punishable by fines and litigation..."

Salem's face twisted in frustration. "Fuck me! You appreciate nothing but your fucking conformity," he balked to no one present. "Where's Adolf Hitler when you need him to snap his fingers and make you fuckers goose step and Sieg heil and drop the facade so everyone can see your true colors!"

Bursting from the table, he stormed to the back patio, flung the screen door open, and screamed into the sprawling sea of beige stucco houses.

"Fuck you, you fuckin drones and clones! Leave me the fuck alone!"

A few hours later, Salem found himself parked on the shoulder of a highway, sandwiched between two cop cars with their lights flashing. Two highway patrolmen circled the graffiti car, one pointing out various details as the other jotted notes in a notebook. A tow truck waited to haul the car away. In a kind of nightmare of disbelief, Salem watched it all unfold with a mix of sadness and bitterness.

* * *

Back in the here and now on Amtrak, Salem sat in his seat in coach, deep in thought. He reached into his bag, retrieved a Styrofoam cup, and poured himself wine from a five-liter box of cabernet. Across from him sat a lean redheaded man in his mid-20s, dressed in a light blue V-neck sweater. His name was Buzz.

"And that was that," Salem said, finishing his story.

Buzz tilted his head, intrigued. "That's it?"

Salem looked out the window, his gaze distant. "No, that isn't it. But that was it for me and cars. That sad beauty was my first and last. Then it was back to riding trains with a vengeance. Want some wine?"

"Yes, I would love some."

Salem poured wine into another cup for Buzz.

Buzz sipped, then asked, "So you never got your car out of impound?"

"Actually, I did." Salem told how he had paid a disheveled and grease-stained man at an impound yard and retrieved his keys.

"Then I went home, loaded a backpack full of clothes, grabbed all my cash and jumped back in the front seat. I had noticed an unpleasant odor on the drive back from the junkyard and now discovered the source. I had figured a homeless guy had slept in the car, but no it was worse. Someone, maybe the scurvy bastard impound guy or a cop had actually taken a shit in the backseat. Nice huh? The artistic expression of the hoi polloi, creative but limited."

Salem went on to tell how he drove several hours out into the Mojave Desert near California City.

"I stopped a few hundred yards from the main east west railroad corridor. I lifted the hood, pulled the lid off the air cleaner, and filled it with gasoline to make it look like an engine fire. Standing back, I blew the car a kiss before tossing a match."

"Then what?!"

"I walked away South occasionally glancing over my shoulder at the flames. In the distance, I saw a freight train. By a stroke of luck it was crawling along and even slowed down as it neared me. I got a running start, jumped on and away I went."

Back on the train, Buzz shook his head, incredulous.

"Jesus. That was a helluva statement, man."

Salem stared out the window, lost in his thoughts. The Amtrak glided through another generic town, the landscape dominated by familiar brand names—Pizza Hut, McDonald's, Burger King, Applebee's, Hollywood Video—rearranged from the last town but all the major corporate brands present and accounted for.

"Statement? That was no statement. I'm just not a fighter. I've been hammered on by so-called normal society and normal people my whole life. Most people think growing up means surrendering to the nine-to-five, the cubicle prison. But that just never worked for me. And every time I open my mouth in opposition of this norm I get called judgmental, egotistical, an asshole or a slacker. Between that and the constant criticism my writing evokes, I'm very tired."

Buzz, sitting nearby, scanned the aisle for an excuse to leave.

"Well, thanks for the wine," Buzz said, rising. "I'm gonna get back to my seat, make sure my stuff is all there. See you later in the bar maybe?"

Salem nodded. "Sure. See ya."

He watched Buzz walk away, then turned back to face forward. "I have happy stories, too," he said to himself. "A few, anyway."

Pouring himself more wine, Salem leaned back and sipped. A tear escaped from behind his sunglasses, trailing down his face. "Hold it together, man," he muttered to himself. "Enough bad memories for one day." But more tears fell. He gritted his teeth and slammed his head sideways against the window. "Happy thoughts," he hissed with a slam. "Happy thoughts!"

Pulling out his stash of pills, Salem selected a red capsule and swallowed it. He leaned back, closing his eyes.

When Salem's eyes opened again, he found himself standing at the front of the coach car dressed in a bright red tailcoat with gold detailing, a crisp white shirt, black top hat, and polished boots. The seats faced him, each one occupied by a distinct figure—a surreal parade of careers: a tool salesman, a nurse, a preacher, a plumber, and many others. It was a Noah's Ark of occupations.

He began walking down the aisle, tapping individuals on the shoulder as he spoke. From somewhere carnival music filled the car.

"Ladies and gentlemen, welcome to Never Never Land! They don't call it a train of thought for nothing. The train is steady! A straight-shooting lullaby! A poet's dream. The only way to fly! It's what I was born for, just like you, sir, were born to sell tools, and you tires, you real estate, and you pills. Just like you were meant to nurse, you to build, you to broker, and you to breed. Just like you were born to plot, to plumb, to preach, to fight, to fish, to fuck..."

Reaching the end of the car, Salem spun around, arms raised. The passengers turned in their seats to watch him. There was a long pause as they hung on his next word. But Salem appeared to lose his train of thought. At last, he shouted, "Whatever, people! Just know this! Be you a porn star or a pulpit-pounding instrument of God, you are not ME!"

Salem's eyes opened again, this time to the so-called real world. He was back from the dream, back in his seat in the present, groggy. The aisle was empty, and the career-people were gone. Across from him, an elderly couple slept, the old man snoring softly. Salem's eyes fluttered closed again.

❋ ❋ ❋

Salem drifted back now to 1985. The train wound through the forested wilderness of the Rocky Mountains. Outside, a swollen, icy river glimmered in the moonlight. Inside, the car's dimmed lights created a hushed ambiance, broken only by the dovelike cooing and kisses of lovers.

Salem, now in his late teens, lay sprawled across two seats with a petite young Noni. Her long, straight dark hair cascaded down her back to her waistline. A ballerina, she had the body of an athlete and the face of a sleepy seraph.

"You smell like Christmas and sweet sexy sweat," he murmured. "Like angels and babies and rain."

"Mmm, you're really hard," she replied.

"No wonder, with you squeezing it like that," Salem groaned. "Look at those women over there. I think they can see what you're doing. Maybe we should go downstairs?"

Salem had noticed that the ladies across the aisle were taking notice of their all-but-fourth base love play. He took her hand, leading her down the narrow hall. He winked mischievously at the ladies as they passed.

The teenagers slipped into the ladies changing room and locked the door. The space was cramped but twice as big as the men's toilet and featured a long counter with two sinks, surrounded by makeup lights. A cushioned bench lined the back wall.

The two embraced with almost violent intensity. While kissing, the girl unbuttoned Salem's jeans, pushing his pants down over his hip bones, sat him back on the bench, and went down on him.

"This... is my... first time," he breathed. She looked up at him, smiling.

Salem's vision blurred. In his mind, he rode a giant cobra snake as it sped down a dirt track through dense, wet forests of evergreens and into a tunnel.

In the tunnel, the snake glowed fiery red. It began to buck and heave like a bull with a rider.

Suddenly the snake shrank, and they exited the tunnel into light— it was the light of the changing room.

Salem was astride the girl Noni now bent over the counter, her hands pressed against the glass as she moaned and bucked beneath him.

Her whimpers fell in rhythm with the ever-audible clickity-clack of the train on the tracks. Salem pulled her long hair back, and she stared back at him hard in the mirror, her intense hazel eyes burning bright.

Now Noni was up on the counter, seated, her back against the mirror, her legs in the air. Salem heaved into her again and again until he cried out, his whole body a whip snap rigid rod consuming lightning. He collapsed on the girl, his head against the mirror, his eyes closing.

✳ ✳ ✳

Back in the here and now, in the dark behind his eyelids, someone kissed him on the cheek. He turned to see a striking young woman sitting beside him. Her jet-black hair framed porcelain skin, dark eyes, pouting lips and ring-bearing nose. She wore full-body flower-print long johns under a black leather jacket, no pants, just her long john bottoms. A Star of David hung from her neck, and a copy of *Breakfast at Tiffany's* rested in her lap.

The rhythmic clickity-clack of the train filled the silence.

"What didja do that for?" Salem asked, his words slurred and in no way angry.

"You looked like you could use it," she replied.

"Wow. Every time I open my eyes there's somebody new sitting next to me."

"That's train travel," Jackie quipped. "People get on, people get off. I'm Jackie."

Salem lifted his sunglasses and took a peek at Jackie.

"I think I'm glad you got on, Jackie."

Jackie swallowed a pill, washing it down with water. Salem narrowed his eyes. "What was that?"

Feigning innocence, she stuck out her tongue to reveal a red tablet. "Er-ko-anne."

"Percodan?!" Salem's face lit up. "Ooh, now I know I'm glad you got on. I hope you brought enough to share, young lady."

"From the sound of your voice and as passed out as you were," Jackie said, "I'd say you've got something of your own, maybe something better! It's always nicer to eat someone else's." Jackie laughed, handing him a pill.

Salem popped it without water and stared out the window. "Are you feeling in the Christmas spirit, Jackie?" he asked.

"You're kidding, right?"

"No."

"I'm Jewish, as if you hadn't guessed."

Salem eyed her attire. "You're the damnedest lookin' Jew I've ever seen. Do all good Jewish girls travel in their underwear?"

Jackie smirked, her tone playful. "You like my undies?"

"I do."

Switching from flirty to serious, Jackie asked, "Do you have a girlfriend?"

"I do not."

"Family?"

"Yeah."

"Where at?"

"My father and half-brother Pierre are in Paris. My mother lives in Arizona."

"Who are you closest to?"

"None of them."

"Oh, come on." Jackie poked him.

"My brother, I guess. He's great. But he was raised in France, so we're a lot different. He calls our coffee 'American sock juice.' Nobody can hurl insults like the French."

Salem peered down at Jackie's mismatched socks, one forest green, one yellow. "Speaking of which, I like your socks."

"Conformity is the jailer of freedom," she said with pride.

"I see. Yes, assuredly." Then after a pause while they both stared at her socks, Salem continued, "I'm sure that's what Kennedy meant. Socks."

"Why aren't you spending Christmas with your brother?"

"Who says I'm not?"

"Just a feeling," Jackie said, pausing to stare at him. "Something about you. Something dark. Something says you're not going to be spending Christmas with anyone... anymore."

Salem turned to her and stared long and hard, his expression unreadable. After a long silence, he asked, "Ever witnessed death, Jackie?"

Jackie went from serious to animated in a half second. "There was this thing I saw on one of those true death videos, about this woman who went swimming in this lake right next to a nuclear plant. She came out of the water screaming, and she had this giant leech on her arm."

Jackie gestured, measuring out a basketball-sized leech, her big eyes growing all the wider.

"They couldn't get it off her! So they had to cut off her arm, and she ended up dying anyway because the leech was all toxic!"

"Thrilling," Salem said with a sigh. "Jesus, I'm getting painfully sober. Join me in some wine?"

Pouring two glasses from the box of cabernet, Salem handed one to Jackie.

"You got a better story?" she asked.

He stared out the window, lost in thought. "I do, in fact. Oh, do I ever. Buckle your seatbelt, Dorothy."

❊ ❊ ❊

It was 1992. The cafe car of a passenger train buzzed with activity. At the far end, Salem, 25 years old, fresh-faced with short blond hair and handsome in an olive-green wool sweater, spoke with a conductor. The conductor shook his head, gestured toward a booth, and said a few words drowned out by the din of the packed car.

Salem approached the indicated booth. Two uniformed conductors sat across from Dougie Souza, a rugged, jovial train engineer in his late 40s. Dougie's dark sunglasses and Marlboro Man aura commanded attention. The men were mid-laughter when Salem interrupted, addressing Dougie directly.

"Hi. Excuse me gentlemen. Name's Salem," he said. "I've been on the train since L.A. I'm writing about train travel and was hoping to get to ride shotgun before we hit Boston." When none of the men laughed, Salem knew he was in.

Minutes later, Salem was seated with Dougie and the conductors. The conversation was lively, with Dougie holding court. His thick New York accent cut through the noise as he shared stories from his two decades on the rails. Salem jotted notes in a steno pad, his face occasionally betraying discomfort as they shared gruesome stories.

"You bet," Dougie said, grinning. "Couple of cows, a truck, a bus—both empty, mind you—a bunch of shopping carts, railroad ties, a refrigerator."

"A refrigerator?" one conductor exclaimed. "Jesus!"

The other conductor clearly hailed from south Boston. Mocking a domestic scene, he adopted a high-pitched voice. "No suppa tonight, hon. Little Barry and his buddies fed the Frigidaire to the train."

Dougie laughed. "This one woman passenger, she's drunk, right? She detrains at a fuel stop. When the conductor whistles our departure, she comes running out of the bar, finds herself on the wrong side of the train, and decides to crawl under."

The first conductor shook his head in protest. "Oh, I don't wanna hear this!"

Salem stopped writing, his expression turning green as Dougie continued. "I start rolling, not knowing she's there. Well… she lost both her left arm and her left leg." Dougie paused for effect, then delivered the punchline. "She's all right now."

"Ohhhwww!" the men roared, the table erupting with groans.

"In twenty years, I've never killed anyone," Dougie said, his tone more serious. "But we've seen it plenty, ha guys? It's never pretty. You know what happens to people hit by a train going over forty?

People shatter." He turned to Salem, patting him on the shoulder and locking eyes.

"Don't worry kid. I'm a crippler, not a killer."

Outside, the silver train adorned with red, white, and blue stripes shuddered to a stop. Salem and Dougie had de-trained and now walked alongside the long string of cars, past four engines, until they reached the front. Together, they climbed aboard.

Inside the engine room, the space was stark and cramped, painted entirely in pea green except for the red cushion on the engineer's chair. Salem settled into a high seat by the left-side window, his view dominated by the flat windshield, the tracks ahead, and the train's snub nose.

Dougie grinned as he pressed a green button. "Here we go!"

The train began to move. Salem cheered. "Yee-hah!"

Half an hour later, Salem grinned ear to ear as the train

sped through pastures, glided through a small town, and barreled through a forest. Inside the engine, Dougie and Salem talked animatedly, their laughter ringing above the roar of the locomotive. At some point, Salem noted the speed on the digital readout: 75mph.

The mood shifted as Dougie's face suddenly went pale. Salem followed his gaze to the tracks ahead.

Salem squinted, leaning forward. "Hey, what the…?"

Dougie's voice was tense. "Fuck."

Ahead, a woman in a light blue dress stood motionless on the tracks, directly in the train's path. The roaring engine fell silent in Salem's mind as he processed the surreal sight.

The woman struck a match, lit a cigarette clenched between her lips, took a long drag, and exhaled. She slowly turned to face the oncoming train.

"No," Salem whispered, his voice barely audible.

Reality snapped back with the deafening roar of the locomotive. The woman vanished beneath the steel snout of the train less than ten feet from the men, followed by a horrible slamming thud. The brakes screeched, and Dougie's scream tore through the air.

"Fuuuuuuuuukkkk!"

❈ ❈ ❈

Back in the here and now, Salem's head slammed against the window as the train lurched violently to one side as its brakes screeched through a sharp curve. Gritting his teeth, he threw out his arms to brace himself.

He leapt up from his seat, spilling wine and dropping his steno pad onto the floor. Climbing over Jackie, he muttered urgently, "Excuse me! Gotta get some air."

Jackie, startled, watched him grab his steno pad and go.

Salem bolted down the stairs to the lower level, tore open the window and stood there breathing deeply. A sign on the window read:

OPENING WINDOW STRICTLY PROHIBITED!

The wind rushed passed as he stared into the impenetrable darkness outside. After a few deep breathes inhaled and held, he closed the window, sat down on the floor by the door and began to write.

Even the moon is in on the dream. Aware. It knows where I'm headed and hides its face in fear. I'd swear it was out there when was it.. yesterday? Now only the black of forbidding night. Even the moon is in on the dream. Aware. It knows where I'm headed and hides its face in fear. I'd swear it was out there... when was it, yesterday? Now only blackness.

Salem climbed back up the spiral staircase and began walking the length of the darkened train. His steps were careful but uneven, adjusting to the gentle sway of the moving cars. The dim floor lights resembled a runway, casting faint glows as he passed. The verse he had composed ran over in his head.

We cut through this blackness with terrific speed, wrapped in a thousand tons of steel. Such frailty, such power. Frailty and power, chaos disguised as order.

Up in the cockpit of the train, the lone engineer sat bathed in the glow of his instruments. His eyes fluttered closed, his head nodding forward, only for consciousness to jolt him awake again moments later. Sleep crept back relentlessly.

Seventeen-hundred asses on the line at 90 mph screaming across the world and surrendered, all of us, to the train. Blindly faithful, we rely on one man to get us to Christmas alive.

Salem continued his trek through car after car, passing through double doors, navigating narrow aisles, and making his way forward. The train was a holiday train, a titan, stretching for dozens of cars. Maximum capacity.

The rhythmic sounds of the train provided a backdrop for his introspection.

I knew such a man. A competent man. But chaos is merciless. It respects no man.

He paused mid-stride, lost in thought.

Did I tell Jackie my story? No. She struck me as the type who would freak at the introduction of such harsh realities into her pill-popping world. I understood all this too well and so spared her my hell.

His face tightened as memories surfaced.

My own pill habit began the day the woman in blue met her death and threw my already tenuous grasp on reality and growing sense of unease and alienation with the world into mad, psychic overdrive.

Salem shook his head, as if trying to physically push the thoughts away, and kept walking, the dark train stretching endlessly ahead. The thoughts and memories came anyway.

Salem sat trackside wrapped in a wool blanket, an Emergency Medical Technician at his side. The EMT opened a bottle, handed him two large pills, and gave him a reassuring pat on the back as Salem swallowed them.

First, it was counseling. Tell me about the accident. Tell me about your parents' divorce. And you drink how much?

He pictured himself slumped in a high-back chair, talking to a counselor who nodded and frowned sympathetically.

Then they start throwing the drugs at you. The inhibitors—

monoamine oxidase and selective serotonin reuptake: Prozac, Paxil, Zoloft, Wellbutrin, Norpramin, Prednisone. You name it.

The Amtrak aisle-walking Salem chuckled aloud as his imagination toyed with memories. A psychiatrist loomed in his memory, leaning into a medicine cabinet and pulling out bottles. His imagination gave the psychiatrist a mad scientist face as the man started tossing pill bottles over his shoulder at Salem one by one. Each label flashed vividly in his mind. Diazepam, Lorazepam, Alprazolam, Clonazepam.

Tell them you have anxiety attacks, and they'll dope you up on benzos. Migraines? Have some codeine, Percodan, Darvocet. Ooh got a really bad one? Go to the hospital for shots of Imitrex and Demerol. Pretty soon, you don't know if you are transparent or thick as a brick, muscle and skin or ectoplasmic goo.

Salem remembered stumbling into an emergency room, his head in his hands. He remembers himself bent over for a shot in the ass, followed by walking out dazed and stoned on Demerol, his 4 foot 11" girlfriend struggling to support him as they stumbled giddily up their apartment staircase.

Salem rounded a corner and descended another staircase to that car's lower level. He walked down the short hall to the bathrooms, opened a door, and stepped inside.

Pulling a pill bottle from his jacket, he set it down on the counter. He splashed cold water on his face, then opened the bottle, tipped it to his mouth, and swallowed the first thing that came out. As he tucked the bottle back into his jacket, he turned to the mirror, flashing himself a Cheshire Cat grin.

But you do know one thing quite well, don't you Salem? As long as we've got our stash, everything's gonna be just fine. Sit back, relax, Mr. Salem. Take your jacket off. Take your shoes off. Take your head off. One pill makes you larger, one pill makes you small. Down the rabbit hole we go. Welcome to Never Never Land.

When Salem exited the bathroom, he saw a conductor standing by the open train door. The chill of the night air hit him immediately.

The train had stopped.

"Where the hell are we?" Salem asked.

"Minot," the conductor replied. "We'll be here for an hour. But be careful. Stray too far from the train, and you *mi- not* make it back."

Salem gave the man a skeptical look. "Hmm. Funny."

Buzz appeared from the stairwell. Salem visibly brightened.

"Hey, what's the buzz, Buzz?" Salem called out with a grin. "Looks like we've got an open door into another dimension. A tear in the very fabric of reality. Up for some adventure? Tear up the town? Mr. Conductor here says if we venture too far, however, we might not make it back from Minot. Ooooh!"

The train loomed in the distance now, a dark silhouette against the barren urban landscape of Minot, North Dakota. Salem and Buzz trudged through the empty lots and streets, warmly dressed against the biting cold of the winter night. The orange glow of streetlights cast long shadows as they walked.

"What's your story, Buzz?" Salem asked, breaking the silence. "Where you from? Where are you going? What's your passion? I hope I didn't spook you too much earlier."

Buzz glanced at Salem his expression unreadable. "That's a lot of questions. I'm from Canada. I'm going to New York to see my daughter. She is my passion. After my daughter, there's my sculpture. And yes, you did spook me earlier."

Salem stopped, visibly startled. "No! I'm sorry, how?"

Buzz hesitated before answering. "I dunno. You just seemed dangerously depressed, and I'm too on edge myself lately to deal with that. All the time, I live in fear of losing my daughter since her mother took her so far away."

"I'm sorry to hear that," Salem said sincerely. "Point taken. I shall resist the dark side of the force, at least tonight. You have my word."

They walked on in near silence, the quietude punctuated by their footsteps as they approached a convenience store.

The trouble was, Salem figured, the dark side of the force had crept into his veins years ago, and all he reckoned he could do to keep from crying was pop pills and hope no one noticed the shadow. Like everyone, he wanted to be free to talk about his fears. But he could see that with Jackie and Buzz, as with so many other people his age, fear was rampant. The only thing people had to keep themselves from melting down in the presence of someone else's dark voodoo were pretend happy thoughts and denial.

Glancing at Buzz, Salem made up his mind in that moment to raise the spirits of everyone he met on the train in a last, likely-too-late effort to save himself.

Do you read, Buzz?"

"Some."

"I read a lot. I just read an essay by a guy named Sherman Alexie. He said a smart Indian is a dangerous person. Alexie was a smart Indian kid which I guess ain't cool amongst natives. So, kids made fun of him and the tribe feared him. I related to that. Being a poet in the states is like being a smart Indian, maybe. It's like a four letter word. Even 'writer' is a conversation killer. Soon as people learn I'm not famous, may as well have said I'm dying of cancer. If you're not already famous in your twenties, what are the chances right? Slim to none."

"Better in the U.S. than anywhere else, probably," Buzz replied.

"Oof. You got me there Buzz."

Inside the Stop By-N-Buy Gas Mart, the fluorescent lights were harsh, casting an unnatural light on the sparse selection of items making everything seem 2-dimensional. Karen, the cashier, stood behind the counter, her coke-bottle glasses magnifying her own flat affect. Salem and Buzz browsed the shelves.

Salem lifted the lid on a pot of soup, took a sniff, and smiled. "Is this homemade?"

It seemed reasonable to Salem that a North Dakota mini mart with pheasants on the walls could reasonably have a couple of moonlighting grandmothers holed up in the back whipping up homemade soup for the patrons of Dinosaur Gas.

"No," Karen replied flatly. "It comes from a baeag."

"A what?" Salem asked, frowning.

"A baeaeaeag!" she repeated.

Buzz chuckled. "A bag. She said it comes from a bag. Bagged soup."

Apparently, being from Canada, Buzz had some insider knowledge on North Dakota vernacular and bagged soup. It smelled like Grandma had made it, and that was good enough for Salem.

Outside the store, Salem walked while slurping his soup. Buzz followed, empty-handed.

"Nothing for you, huh?" Salem asked between bites.

Buzz shook his head. "Nah. Not hungry."

They wandered through the barren streets and lots, the persistent orange glow of Minot's streetlights above them. The winter sky stretched wide and empty, a cold , dark canopy over the quiet town. Buzz and Salem made their way down a set of stairs and across another lot, heading back toward the train.

Minot, Salem thought. What a weird place.

"This place is weird, huh? What a weird reality we detrained into. The quantum physics parallel world theory isn't some element of fantasy like unicorns or trolls but instead derives from oddities in our everyday life and the plausibility of concurrent experiences through the looking glass," Salem offered.

"I don't follow," Buzz replied.

"Think about it. You stumble off a train and out into the chilly night and... I mean a train is a kind of parallel reality unto itself, right? So you detrain into the night and into some bizarro mini-mart on the perimeter of the twilight zone where a local newspaper tells you you're in Minot. And ding! A bell goes off in your brain, and you remember a conductor in a dream telling you that you might not get back to the train if you get off in Minot. And suddenly it's clear. You have stepped off an opiate dream train, a train made of smoke and mirrors and into a reality of your own creation."

'Whoa," Buzz surmised. "You are a trip, eh?"

They passed the Minot Municipal Auditorium, its quiet facade adding to the surreal stillness of the town. There wasn't a human anywhere to be seen nor a moving vehicle.

"Did you ever wonder why all the so-called crazy people say they come from another planet? Xenon and shit. Like that sci-fi writer who started his own religion in the 50s. And definitely street people. Lots of them."

"Huh," Buzz replied. "Yeah, that's more an American thing. We don't really have street people in Canada."

"No? None? Okay, well, I mean you've thought about it, right? How you must be from another planet because everybody here is fucking nuts, right? No?"

Buzz shook his head and shrugged his shoulders.

"Geez. Well, okay sticking to Earth, did you ever stop and think how random it is that we are from where we are from? That we live where we live? Have you ever visited someplace and thought, I could live here. I could move here right now. But you don't for whatever reason. I mean how weird it is that we all live on the same planet and yet people live just such vastly different lives? Back on our home planets we all signed up for the same Earth Vacation package, so what the hell? How come everybody's vacation is so different?

"I thought you said only crazy people came from another planet?" Buzz asked.

"Well! Salem shrugged.

Buzz chuckled.

"If the straight jacket fits," Salem said.

They walked a minute in silence. The Minot Sheriff Station came into view.

"It be strange if we did miss the train, eh?" Buzz asked.

"Yeah," Salem replied, grinning. "Very strange. Maybe Karen would take us in, feed us baeaeagged soup."

They both laughed at the long drawn out vowel sound.

"So, I moved to Minot," Salem began, adopting a mock North Dakota accent based on what he'd heard from Karen. "I set up house, got myself a little Minot woman named Meg and knocked her up."

"Maaag," Buzz said.

"Exactly. So me and Meg we lived on soup from a bag. I got me a job at the bagged soup factory. Worked my way up from bagger to tagger to oh-what-a-dragger, aka manager. Saved up my pennies and eventually bought Bagged Soup, Incorporated. Through proper money management and a little luck, I eventually bought up most of the town despite those who said I might not.

I became sheriff, too, to vindicate Hunter S. Thompson, and later, mayor of Minot."

They stopped in front of a massive retaining wall, twenty feet high and one of many in the area, as though the town had been built on a man-made mountain. The wall was a rock climber's dream, a perfect practice wall. A sign on the wall read:

CLIMBING ON THIS WALL STRICTLY PROHIBITED

Salem smirked. "I bet they don't get many challengers."

"When you become mayor, I'll take over as sheriff and climb that wall whenever I damn well please," Buzz asserted.

"Buzz! My hero. Naturally, you'd have to shoot any punks who tried to climb it without paying you protection money, though?"

Salem laughed, then shouted in a thick German accent, "Ya-voll! Das ist mein fucking vall!"

They both burst out laughing.

"That's what happens when you give an artist a gun and a little authority," Buzz said.

Salem grinned. "Look what it did for Hitler."

Salem and Buzz stepped aboard and climbed the stairs to the second level of the coach car just as the train began to move again.

"Goodnight, Buzz," Salem said.

Buzz smiled. "Hey, that was fun. See you in the morning."

Salem made his way back to his seat, where Jackie was fast asleep. Carefully, he stepped over her legs and settled into the window seat. He put on his headphones and stared out the window. As the outskirts of Minot rolled by in the dark, the gravelly voice of Tom Waits filled his ears and caressed his auditory cortex.

Blow wind blow, wherever you may go, Put on your overcoat, take me away. You gotta take me on into the night, take me on into the night, blow me away, blow me away. I ride upon a field mouse, I was dancing in the slaughterhouse and it was swing along the beltway, you skid along there all day, 'cause I went a little crazy and I sat upon a high chair, and I'm smokin like a diesel way out here.

Outside, the stars glittered brightly against the moonless sky. The outlines of mountains of sand, gravel, and towering industrial elevators emerged momentarily from the shadows before vanishing back into the darkness. A massive blue star appeared, outlined in Christmas lights, advertising a sand and gravel company. It shone brightly, surreal against the stark night.

In the engine room of the Amtrak train, the lone engineer sat slumped in his chair, sound asleep. His mouth hung open, and soft snores filled the cramped space. Slowly, his body began to tilt to one side—first barely noticeable, then gradually faster— until he toppled out of the chair and hit the floor with a thud. The pressure-sensitive mechanism beneath the engineer's chair registered the loss of his weight. Immediately, an alarm blared in the small cabin, and the train's acceleration cut sharply.

Startled awake, the engineer scrambled back into his seat, his eyes wide and breathless. He gripped the controls and brought the train back up to speed. His chest rose and fell as he caught his breath, inhaling deep shaky breaths of relief. Reaching into his pocket, he pulled out a prescription bottle, shook a pill into his hand, and swallowed it dry.

The next day, the Great Plains stretched endlessly beneath a cold blue sky. Cows milled by the tracks, their breath visible in the chilly air. The red-and-white gate lowered over a rural road, holding back a few idling early-model American cars. Exhaust from their tailpipes whirled and swirled and danced on the wind, giving the lifeless vehicles an animated appearance like it was summer and they were all overheating and ready to blow. In truth it was -20F below with the wind-chill.

The train approached at thirty miles per hour, its sheer size dominating the otherwise flat landscape. It was a long, double-decker passenger train trailing freight cars, the rhythmic *clickity-clack* of its wheels echoing through the stillness. After five engines and twelve cars passed, the idling commuters were treated to Salem, Jackie and Agnes all squeezed halfway out of an open boarding door window. Their laughter and screams filled the air as they waved merrily to the barren plains and ghost cars. The idling cars remained frozen amidst the exhaust steam, devoid of visible signs of life from within.

Inside the lower level of the coach car, Salem, Agnes, Jackie, and Buzz pulled themselves back inside and slid the window shut. Jackie and Agnes giggled uncontrollably.

"Hey, sister," Jackie said, catching her breath. "I'm Jackie."

"Agnes," she replied, extending a hand. "Pleased to meet cha!"

Salem gestured toward Buzz, who was crouched over with his ear pressed to a bathroom door. "Jackie, Agnes, the peeping tom over here is Buzz."

Buzz put a finger to his lips and motioned for them to come closer.

He pointed toward the bathrooms with one hand, the other making the shush sign of forefinger on lips. The group tiptoed down the hall, careful not to make a sound. There were four toilet closets, each with a sink, and at the end of the hall, a changing room marked with a feminine symbol on the door.

Muffled noises filtered through the changing room door—the masculine grunts and high-pitched cooing of lovemaking. Suddenly wide-eyed with surprise, Jackie and Agnes stifled their laughter, covering their mouths as they tried to keep quiet.

The group backed around the corner, where Jackie and Agnes immediately erupted into giggles. Agnes began pantomiming a doggie-style scene, playfully mounting the much smaller Jackie.

"I'm your Bunny burning hot coal furnace steam locomotive of love!" Jackie teased, her voice exaggerated.

Agnes grabbed her hips, playing along. "Yeah? Well, get ready for my caboose, baby! Ung! Ung! Ung!"

"Ooh! Ooh! Caboose me, caboose me!" Jackie cried, laughing so hard she nearly fell over.

A conductor's voice crackled over the train's PA system, interrupting their antics.

"Good afternoon, ladies and gentlemen. The dining car is now open. Those of you who would like to join us for lunch, please come to the dining car now. We are presently crossing the Great Plains. The dwellings you see out your window are all part of the Blackfoot Indian Reservation. The Blackfoot are the..."

Salem shook his head. "How come you can say 'Indian Reservation,' but now you have to call the people Native Americans?"

"Who knows," Jackie said, waving it off. "Anyone for lunch? I'm starved. Eww! Who cut one?"

"That would be me," Agnes admitted with a teethy grin. "Sorry. Still hungry?"

Salem grinned. "Buzz?"

Buzz had opened the window again, his head sticking out as he gazed at the landscape rolling by. He didn't respond right away.

"In a minute," he finally said, lost in thought.

"You two girls go get a table and get acquainted," Salem suggested. "We'll be right behind ya."

"Be good," Agnes said with a wink, nodding toward the changing room as she and Jackie left.

Buzz leaned against the open window, staring at the scenery. The flat plains stretched on forever, interrupted by occasional signs of human habitation.

"I love American women," Buzz said, pulling his head back inside.

"Yeah? What's wrong with Canadian women?" Salem asked, joining him.

"Nothing. Just… crazy girls like Jackie and Agnes, they're so… uniquely American."

A UPS truck zoomed past in the distance, a familiar sight against the otherwise bleak landscape. Nearby, several 1970s-era white trailer homes huddled together in a makeshift cul-de-sac, their rooftops weighed down with dozens of old tires to keep them from blowing off in the fierce plains' winds.

Salem smirked. "I dunno. My first girlfriend in college was from British Columbia, and she was totally whacked, but gawd was she hot. She told me I was going to be the first man to ever give birth. She was convinced. At seventeen, that sure blew my mind."

Buzz chuckled. "Did she try to get you pregnant?"

"No, Buzz, as a matter of fact, she did not. I was still a virgin at eighteen, thanks to her. On my birthday, right, she gets me naked and rides me to her own orgasm—with her panties on. Awful tease."

"Awful," Buzz echoed with mock sympathy.

The two young men gazed out at the empty plains as the rhythmic *clickety-clack* of the train played on.

Buzz and Salem walked through the café car on their way to the dining car. Formerly concerned with hiding it, Salem now carried his box of cabernet tucked under his arm.

As they passed through, Salem stopped abruptly at the sight of Lynsie. Entranced, he sat down and watched her. Petite and lovely, dressed like a librarian, she entertained a few children by coloring on scratch-off paper. With a butter knife, she carved tiny cave-art designs—fish, a sun, a stick figure, a lizard—into the black wax, revealing vibrant rainbows beneath.

Her hands moved with delicate precision. Almost translucent, they fascinated Salem. Later he would write:

Blue veins shining through, skin nearly transparent—hands softer than any I'd ever felt. Watching them pull color from darkness like magic, riveting. Cave art drawn by an angel, in a setting no caveman could have dreamed. He dreamt of the hunt, of fire, of sex, of bigger and better caves. But could he have ever imagined the likes of a train?

Just then, a freight train roared past in the opposite direction. Lynsie grabbed the children's hands and pressed them to the vibrating glass. Salem and Buzz exchanged glances and followed, their palms meeting the trembling surface.

Flying across land in a glass and steel cave, feeling the violent burst of air through a water-like barrier, shapes of steel and color flashing past in an indecipherable blur. Never, I'd tell the caveman. Never. To the primitive man, this is Never Never Land.

In the dining car, Jackie, Agnes, and Agnes' boyfriend Eric occupied a booth. Eric, a skinny youth with dreadlocks and a tie-dyed shirt, sat stiffly, looking uncomfortable with the group. Agnes and Eric made a very odd couple.

Salem, Buzz, and Lynsie joined them, squeezing into the booth. Buzz inhaled deeply. "I smell turkey!"

Jackie rolled her eyes. "Really? I smell Target. This whole train stinks of Target."

Salem chuckled. "Everybody, this is Lynsie."

"Hi, Lynsie," Jackie, Agnes, and Eric greeted in unison.

Agnes extended a hand. "Lynsie, I'm Agnes, and this is Eric."

"Hey, guys," Lynsie replied.

Salem gestured toward Eric. "Eric, I'm Salem, and this is Buzz."

Eric nodded curtly. Salem plopped his box of wine onto the table. "Vino, anyone?"

Jackie, Agnes, Lynsie, and Buzz nodded eagerly, while Eric shook his head. Salem poured the wine into Amtrak plastic Dixie water cups. A sign riveted to the wall above the table read:

CONSUMPTION OF PRIVATE ALCOHOL PROHIBITED

Outside their window stretched an endless expanse of brown, butterscotch and deep purple scrub grasses. The plains were pancake-flat except for occasional hillocks. The sky was a flawless and no doubt frigid blue. Cows grazed not far from the train.

Salem gestured toward the window. "Look out there. What do you see? I see a bunch of hamburgers walking around. What are cows anyway but a bunch of hamburgers-in-waiting? Strip away the hides, de-bone 'em, throw some pickles on 'em, a bun above and below, and pow! You've got a hundred four-legged Quarter Pounders. Throw in some elevator music, a dash of Terry Gilliam, and you've got cheeseburgers. Haha. Get it? Cheese-burgers?"

Jackie shook her head, laughing. "Salem, you need help."

"I believe I am being facetious," Salem replied. "At least I think I am."

Lynsie smirked. "I knew a guy who wouldn't eat vegetables because he once heard a carrot scream while he was shrooming. The only thing he'd eat after that were plain hamburgers without the pickle, and he'd apologize to the ketchup."

Pleasant scents drifted through the car from the kitchen. The smells of hamburger and pea soup and vinaigrette salad dressing met the noses of those in the booth.

Agnes grinned. "Well, I'm a super-size order of fries myself. A greasy, salty-sweet, rutty rail-ridin' Van Gogh potato eater. Anybody hungry?"

Agnes tugged at her neckline to reveal her cleavage and accidentally let slip a nipple. Tucking it back in, she realized the dining car steward was standing over her. "Oops."

"I'm sorry," the steward said dryly, "but you all can't sit in one booth. Only four passengers to a booth." He didn't sound sorry.

Jackie turned on her charm, batting her eyes. "Pleeeaaase? We're all family. You just can't break us up!"

Agnes joined in. "Yeah, pleeeeaasse?"

The steward sighed, visibly tired. "What'll it be?"

Jackie grinned. "Turkey for me."

"Yeah, turkey for me too!" Agnes chimed in.

"Turkey three," Salem added.

"What the hell," Lynsie said. "Turkey, please."

Eric glanced up. "I'll have the vegetarian sandwich."

The steward turned to Buzz. "And for you, sir?"

"Nothing for me, thanks," Buzz replied.

Salem eyed Buzz with concern.

"Drinks?" the steward asked, scanning the group. They all smiled sheepishly, glasses of wine already in front of them. The steward rolled his eyes and walked away.

"Rules," Salem muttered. "Always stupid rules and regulations. And do you think it has anything to do with our safety? No."

"Insurance," Agnes replied convincingly.

"Exactly. Like if this train crashed right now, we'd have any more chance of survival being four to a booth."

"I guarantee there's no such sign in the First-Class club car," Salem said.

"Ack! They're picking on poor people!" Agnes said.

"Peasants in the service of royals have always been unkind to other peasants," Lynsie said.

"Humans are hierarchical," Salem offered.

"I've dated a couple of rich guys and I'm telling you they wouldn't give a crap about us having our own booze in here," Jackie said.

"Good point," Buzz said. "But I think in this case it's just a profit thing. Amtrak wanting to make money off your alcohol dependency, just like movie theaters charge ten times the value for popcorn."

"Well, maybe," Salem said. "But that steward? Classic house negro."

"Salem!" Jackie scolded.

"What?!"

"At least on trains there's none of that illusion-of-security bullshit," Jackie added. "I mean, have you ever seen a seatbelt on a train?"

Eric piped in. "Gosh, can you imagine getting stuck out here in the middle of nowhere?"

Buzz glanced out the window. "I think I'd kinda like it out here."

Agnes laughed. "Eric means a place without Nintendo or movie theaters, speaking of popcorn. Eric has a phobia of empty spaces— what most people call nature. Some hippie, huh?"

Everyone turned to Eric, who said nothing and appeared to be pouting. "So, what's up with Eric, Eric? Have some wine."

"I don't drink," Eric said.

"Bummer. How do you cope?"

"Just fine."

"Isolating, though, huh? Don't you miss the frivolity? I mean, we are one frivolous bunch."

"No. Someday when you're depressed and anxious you'll understand."

"Whoa, soldier," Salem replied. "Go easy there. I'm plenty depressed. I just don't wear it on my sleeve.

Salem smiled, raised his glass of wine. "Here's to emptiness of countryside and mind. If a little scary emptiness is what it takes to save some of the Earth from man's ceaseless mini-mall and subdivision conquest, I say hooray. God bless the Great Plains, then."

"God bless the flat lands, the bad lands," Agnes added.

"Let no man have the courage or desire to live here, to screw it up with manufactured *beauty*," Salem continued.

"Think how quiet it is out there," Buzz added.

"Blissful," Lynsie agreed. "No car alarms, street sweepers, garbage trucks, howling drunks…"

"No howling drunks?" Salem feigned shock.

"To howling drunks!" Agnes shouted, raising her Dixie cup of wine.

The group laughed and raised their cups. "To howling drunks!" they chorused, with Eric remaining silent.

When the steward returned with their food, he handed Salem an open-faced turkey sandwich smothered in gravy, mashed potatoes, and mixed vegetables. Salem inhaled deeply through his nose. "Ahh! Turkey!"

He nudged his plate toward Buzz. "Eat. No arguments."

Buzz hesitated, looking embarrassed, but then took a deep breath, nodded, and picked up his fork.

Salem leaned back in his seat, swirling the wine in his cup as the laughter at the table died down. "You know," he began, "this reminds me of a train trip I took back in college. I was a skinny, broke kid trying to make my way as a writer. I had this sleeper room—it was part of a deal I got for writing about the trip for the *Tribune*. I invited two so-called friends along, Dick and Pete."

"Wait," Jackie interrupted, already grinning. "Their actual names were Dick and Pete?"

"Scouts honor," Salem said, raising his hand. "Anyway, Dick was an arrogant prick who thought the world owed him a living. Always wore a prep school shirt and a ball cap from one resort or another. Pete? He was this big and loud oaf with all the brainpower of a couch cushion, always showing off his high school ring like it was a Superbowl ring."

The table chuckled, and Salem continued. "So there we were in the dining car. They'd ordered this huge pizza and a couple of beers, and I—being the poor starving writer—was just sitting there with my steno pad, watching them eat."

"What'd you do?" Agnes asked, clearly intrigued.

"I said, 'May I please have a slice?' And you know what Dick says to me?"

"What?" Lynsie asked, leaning forward.

"'You got any money?'" Salem shook his head. "Like he didn't already know I was broke. And then Pete—big ole Pete—chimes in with, 'Yeah, you gonna pay up, writer boy?' They both thought it was hilarious."

"What assholes!" Jackie exclaimed.

"Right?" Salem said. "So I looked at Dick and said, 'Come on, Dick. You know how little money I had for this trip. You're not going to share one lousy slice of pizza after I invited you both along? After I let you crash in my sleeper room?'"

"What'd he say?" Buzz asked.

"And Dick—cool as you please—just shakes his head and goes, 'You need to get a real job, boyo. One that pays.'" Salem paused, shaking his head at the memory. "I just stared at him, completely bewildered. Like, really? That's how you're gonna treat me?"

The table was silent for a moment before Jackie raised her glass. "Here's to Dick and Pete," she said. "Wherever they are, may they choke on their pizza."

"Yeah!" Agnes chimed in. "And on one another's dongs as they do their Dick and Peter sixty-nine!"

The group burst out laughing, tapping their cups together. Salem couldn't help but grin. "Thanks, guys," he said, taking a sip of his wine. "It's good to know someone's got my back."

Salem's box of cabernet sat on the table, and everyone but Eric drank from it. Eric sipped orange juice instead, looking out of place. Salem occasionally scribbled notes in his steno pad as the group talked.

Jackie leaned in, her voice conspiratorial. "...so there I am on the train one time and the car I'm in is half empty. I dunno, it was March or something, and this creepy guy gets on the train, walks down, sits right adjacent to me across the aisle and starts wacking off!"

The table erupted in disgust. "Eewww!" Agnes and Lynsie exclaimed in unison.

"What did you do?" Lynsie asked, her face scrunched with revulsion.

Jackie grinned wickedly. "I got up and I smacked him."

"Well," Eric chimed in, "I heard about this guy who got shot with a .22 when someone accidentally shot a gun off on Greyhound."

"Sounds like Greyhound," Buzz said.

"Or urban legend," Agnes said sarcastically. She slammed down her full cup of wine in one gulp.

"Ride the Pooch, get the smooch," Salem said.

"Smooch?" Lynsie asked.

"Yeah smooch, like kiss of death," Salem grinned.

"Uh huh," Jackie said, dragging it out. "As metaphors go, that's a stretch."

Salem turned the conversation back to travel advice. "Okay, guys.

Top ten rail-riding tips for Amtrak newcomers! Number one: find a good seatmate if you can't have a double to yourself. Otherwise, some nasty monster with three heads, halitosis, and a bad speed habit will find you and make your trip a living hell."

Jackie nodded, producing a mace dispenser from her jacket. "Be ready with the mace!" she said, holding it up threateningly.

Agnes chimed in. "Sit far from the doors."

Buzz added, "And not directly upstairs from the shitters."

"Open bathroom doors really slowly," Agnes warned. "Those lock mechanisms were definitely designed by a creep."

They all made awkward faces and nodded in agreement, vividly recalling their own strange encounters.

Eric finally spoke up, quieter than the others. "Take off your shoes and stay awhile," he said, grinning faintly.

Agnes laughed. "Build yourself a fort! Like when we were kids. Hang a blanket down from the luggage rack to shroud your seat area."

Jackie leaned in with a mischievous smirk. "Worst case scenario, puke on the seat beside you. That'll make sure no creeps sit next to you."

Speaking of preventative measures," Lynsie chimed in, "Eat lunch, not dinner if you're on a one-meal-a-day budget. It's the same food at half the price."

Salem grinned at the group. "Okay. And how about supplies? Booze? Food?"

Agnes slurred, "Don't eat yellow snow."

"I say at least two liters of boxed wine per day of travel," Salem declared, "allowing room to share."

"Packaged smoked salmon, water crackers, Swiss cheese," Lynsie added with enthusiasm.

"Eeewww!" Jackie groaned, waving her hand in front of her nose as an unpleasant odor hit the table. Everyone but Eric joined in, waving at the smell.

"She who smelt it dealt it," Agnes said, a hopeful tone in her voice.

"She with swell tits dealt it!" Jackie shouted, pointing at Agnes.

Agnes assumed a teethy grin and half-raised her hand. "I resemble that remark."

"AGNES!" the group groaned in unison.

"You know what Kurt Vonnegut said?" Lynsie asked rhetorically. "We're here on Earth to fart around."

"Du bist ein Furzkanone, Agnes," Salem said. "A fart cannon."

"That's easy for you to say," Agnes said.

Just then Lynsie tipped back her wine but spilled Buzz's glass across the table and onto Salem's steno. Without hesitation, Agnes and Salem dove forward, slurping the spilled wine off the table while the rest of the group cheered.

"Woo hoooo!" Jackie shouted. "Now we know who the future alcoholics are."

The laughter and banter quieted in Salem's mind as his thoughts took over.

Now these are my people, he mused. Five modern-day rail-riding hobos, drunks every one of 'em. Well, almost all of them. I looked around at all of them... Agnes the bullish buxom beauty, Lynsie the waif, Jackie the pill-popping flirt, Buzz the normal guy, and Eric the milquetoast, and I was glad to know them—even though, in reality, I didn't know them at all. That's the beauty of train travel for a guy like me. You make friends fast, and nobody judges you. There isn't time. If only everybody treated life like a two-day train ride. Bing! Bang! Live it up. Tomorrow... who knows?

Unfortunately, whenever Salem went into his thoughts, she stood there waiting for him. He saw the woman in the blue dress stepping onto the tracks, the cigarette rising to her lips. The flame, the red glow, the exhale. The locomotive, huge now, barreling down on her. The sound of the train horn blared in his head, followed by the screeching brakes.

Later, Salem held the door to the deluxe sleeper room open, ushering Jackie, Agnes, Lynsie, and Buzz inside. The tiny room barely accommodated the five of them.

"Come on in, hurry!" he urged, closing the door and drawing the curtain as soon as they were inside.

"What are we doing?" Lynsie asked, her words slurred. "We can't be in here!"

"This is great!" Agnes exclaimed, looking around. "But how do we know no one's staying in this room?"

"Don't worry," Salem assured her. "I stole a look at the conductor's schedule. This room is empty until our next stop—in about three hours."

Lynsie, glassy-eyed, leaned over and kissed Buzz on the cheek. Buzz looked startled but pleased. Jackie raised an eyebrow, a sly smile forming.

"Ooh," she teased. "What was that? Me thinks I smell romance in the air."

Salem grabbed the clean glasses provided with the room, filled them with wine, and handed one to Buzz. "Only two glasses," he said with mock grandeur. "Here's one for the lovebirds. My harem and I shall share the other."

Jackie snorted, pulling out a pipe, a bag of pot, and her battered paperback of *Breakfast at Tiffany's*. She sorted through the buds on the book's cover, packed the pipe, and lit up. Salem raised his glass. "To lovebirds!"

"To staying buzzed!" Jackie added, holding her breath before exhaling a plume of smoke and laughing, coughing.

The room soon filled with smoke and laughter. The pipe made its rounds, and by the time it came back to Jackie, everyone except Salem spoke in slurred, giggly tones.

"Did anyone have a nice Thanksgiving this year?"

"That's random," Agnes said with a cough of smoke.

"Have any of you ever had just like a pleasant chill Turkey Day or Christmas? I am serious. You know, civil and lovely and homey and comfortable and loving as it was pictured by the likes of Norman Rockwell? And not the discordant horror show that results no doubt as a karmic manifestation of the holiday's perverse roots in genocide? You know, welcome to our charnel house of 1000 corpses slaughter and blood-letting ritual?"

Jackie coughed out a smoke ring, shook her head and cackled. "What the fuck Salem?"

"The bloated turkey of manifest destiny. I mean, are we

celebrating our own gluttony and crisp white cottony comfortable life, or are we celebrating conquest over the people who inhabited this land for thousands of years before us? Is either morally correct?" Salem tilted his head in deep thought.

"Man DO NOT give Salem that pipe again!" Agnes said.

"You know after the Civil War the government promised the freed slaves 40 acres and a mule? They didn't get it. Martin Luther King said instead they gave away the whole west to the white peasants of Europe. To populate it. To make a country. To make a white country. Think about that. Then of course blacks got fucked in the post-war suburban boom. We are some racist motherfuckers when you think about it."

All heads nodded then shook from side to side in the smoke.

"I don't feel racist," Agnes said.

"One year at thanksgiving my grandfather got mean ugly with a German exchange student staying with my cousin's family," Jackie said. "He started calling him Jerry right across the table and blamed the kid's family for the Holocaust. It didn't help that the kid's name was Helmut which you know, is just so... German! Of course he topped it all off calling him a Nazi while we were digging into the pie."

"I checked out Mein Kampf from the library once," Buzz said.

"Whoa!" the girls said in unison.

"Hold on a minute, eh?!" Buzz protested. I got it just to try and understand like, what the heck. Everybody in Germany had to own the book. I just wanted to know, was it in there? Yes. The answer is yes. Hitlers whole plan is in there. I was sure some government agency had taken note of the book's withdrawal, you know like how in those conspiracy movies the CIA knows every time somebody checks out Catcher in the Rye. I knew my government wasn't going to arrest me, but I wasn't so sure about yours."

"I read some of it, too, Buzz," Salem said. "Made you feel sick, huh? Me, too. I felt like a million of Jews were screaming at me across the Atlantic and 50 years of time. Jews, Gypsies, the disabled, gay & lesbian people, and anyone who didn't agree with the Nazis. That's the shortlist. Did you ever wonder if that shit would ever happen again?

"I'm bi," Jackie said. "I remember my surprise at learning that in Berlin before Hitler people were openly gay and transgender. I had just assumed that Germans had always been hardcore straight white people."

"Yeah and I'm Jewish ya'll," Lynsie said. "How the hell did we get from Thanksgiving to Nazis?

There was a lull in the conversation until Salem thought of a good way to jump tracks.

"Did you ever hear William Burroughs' Thanksgiving Prayer?" Salem asked. "'Thanks for the American dream to vulgarize and to falsify until the bare lies shine through.'"

"Whoa!" Buzz said.

"I read that!" Jackie said. "I loved the bit about the bitter old white ladies and their mean faces!"

"Oh yeah. Close. Hold on I got the damn thing memorized," Salem said, closing his eyes. He affected a nasally voice with a slow syrupy cadence. "Thanks for decent church-going women with their mean, pinched, bitter, evil faces."

"Wow. That guy could turn a phrase," Lynsie said.

"I'll never forget this friend's 14-year-old daughter telling me her favorite book was Naked Lunch," Jackie said. "I was horrified."

"Oh yeah why?" Lynsie asked.

"Cuz it's like full of kinky gay sex and erotic executions and guy's cumming while being hanged," Agnes said matter-of-factly.

"Okay maybe we should circle back to Nazis," Lynsie said. "Cleaner subject matter."

"Very clean people the Nazis," Buzz added. "And punctual."

"Germans you mean," Salem corrected. "One should never conflate the two. Most Nazis were Germans, but not all Germans were Nazis. I lived there just before the wall came down. Percentage-wise very few Germans were actually Nazis. I disagree with the notion that all Germany knew the full extent of the atrocities and were complicit or turned a blind eye.

"Whoa," Agnes groaned. "That's good. I'm mostly German."

"It will never happen here in the States," Jackie said. "People are too independent. Germans all march in straight lines and follow orders and shit, no offense Agnes. Nobody in the US follows orders. All my friends are anarchists."

"That's cool," Salem said. "Stick with those friends, Jackie. But I'm not so sure. I think it could happen again anywhere. Author Graham Greene called Nazism an abscess that had been lanced. He said that totalitarian poison could still spread to countries which had escaped the first infection."

"Oof," Buzz said. "Like us."

"That's right. Think about all the Holocaust deniers."

"I've heard of those assholes," Lynsie said. "Fuck those people."

"I'm not a betting man, but if I were I'd put money on a whole new Nazi uprising the moment the last Holocaust survivor dies," Salem said.

"What?!! That is crazy talk," Jackie said.

"That's pretty grim, Salem, even for you," Buzz said.

"Okay can we please change the subject or go back to telling Thanksgiving stories?" Lynsie pleaded. "This shit is creeping me out."

Everybody went quiet for what felt like a full minute. The clickity clack of the train returned to consciousness. Salem couldn't help himself and broke the silence with the last line of Burroughs' prayer again, nasally and slow.

"Thanks for the last and greatest betrayal of the last and greatest of human dreams," Salem added.

"Ugh!" the group sighed collectively.

"Sorry," Salem said.

"Okay enough," Jackie shouted. "Who's up for rollerblading down the aisles?"

"Can we do it naked?" Agnes asked. She suddenly let rip a roaring booming laugh.

"Absolutely," Jackie declared.

"Wait!" Lynsie froze, her eyes wide. "I think I hear a conductor!"

The group held their breath. Only the rhythmic *clickity-clack* of the rails broke the silence. After a moment, they all relaxed, and Buzz tickled Lynsie.

"Paranoia, eh!" he teased.

"Speaking of which," Salem said, glancing around, "Where's Eric?"

Agnes shrugged. "Abandoned shit—er, ship," she said with a hiccup.

"Paranoid!" Buzz repeated, grinning.

"More or less," Agnes said nonchalantly.

"I feel like an outlaw," Lynsie said.

"I was an outlaw once," Agnes said.

"Really?!" Lynsie said.

"Stole a cop car."

"What? Whoa!" Jackie said, leaning forward. "Go cowgirl! Do tell! And please don't fart until the end. I don't wanna miss anything when I have to dive out of this coffin and into the aisle."

The others chimed in, urging Agnes to continue. She downed the remaining wine in her glass in a single gulp and cleared her throat. Her voice became steady, suddenly clear and uncharacteristically serious.

"About six years ago, long before Eric, I had another boyfriend named Jack. The nightmare began when Jack joined the army and moved us to Fort Hood, Texas. Jack was great—a real outgoing, fun-loving guy who treated me like an angel. Unfortunately, I was all kinds of messed up."

Agnes stared at the glass in her hand, swirling the wine as she spoke. "Well, when the doctors finally got a hold of me a bit later, they told me I was suffering from.." Here Agnes slowed to emphasize every word. ".. major.. clinical.. chronic.. Depression. Probably due to a chemical imbalance, they said."

Just then another train went by in the opposite direction rattling the windows and putting everyone on edge for the seconds it took to pass at a combined speed of 140 mph. "I was barely able to leave her trailer. I was scared all the time, couldn't go outside, and I hated myself," she admitted. "Looking back, my life was going pretty good up until then or so it seemed, but it didn't matter. Something was seriously wrong."

Her voice grew darker as she recalled the fire ants swarming her legs on the rare occasion that she did go out, the oppressive redneck atmosphere, and the constant artillery fire at night. "I'd lay in bed while Jack was out on maneuvers, listening to bombs shake the trailer. I kept thinking, 'That one was Jack. Jack's been blown to bits.' (long pause) Did you know more troops in the US military die in training than in combat? True story."

The others listened, wide-eyed, as Agnes recounted the summer when her only companion was her growing depression. "One thing kept me from hanging myself alongside the dead coyote the neighbors strung up that summer as if that would keep other coyotes away," she said.

"A tornado."

Already silent in the mad thunderous humming way a train car can be silent when the brain adjusts and tunes out the roar, the room grew quieter still. More electric. Tense.

"You know those horrible noises that come on the radio when there's danger?"

"The Emergency Broadcast System," Buzz offered.

"Yes that. Tornado warnings were all over the radio. It was exciting! Something insane going on in the outside world, not just inside my head. It was the first time I ever heard those noises that there was real danger, not just a test. This time they were talking directly to me. Anyone in trailer homes in such-n-such area, get out immediately and seek shelter elsewhere. This time, as grandpa used to say, the wolf was at the door.

"What did you DO?!"

"Well, I went to the door and opened it."

"Whoa!!" Her audience gasped.

"Right outside I saw two things. One, a pea green blanket sky with like no visibility past 100 yards or so. And two, a cop car idling right beside my mailbox, door open, cop across the road knocking on my neighbor's door. I crossed to the car, got in, hit the gas and in a matter of seconds I was on the farm to market road headed straight into that pea green veil. I knew from somewhere that tornados like to hide behind a soupy sky like that. Mind you my overriding impulse everyday was to end it all. I guess I figured if I was going to die, what better exit than a tornado? Imploded by air pressure 100 times greater than the Earth's gravity and shot up into the sky in a zillion pieces. People felt bad for those space shuttle people and that teacher who died. Not me. We all gotta go sometime. May as well go out on a rocket, and what better rocket than one cooked up by Mother Earth herself? I saw my chance and I took it." Agnes smiled wryly.

"Holy screaming hemorrhoids, Batman," Jackie said, whistling through her teeth in awe. "Then what?!"

Agnes bit her lower lip.

"What? What is it?" Buzz implored.

"I gotta fart," Agnes said.

"NOOOO!" Everyone shouted.

"Quick! Finish the story," Lynsie said, "Then you can fart."

I headed straight for the tornado, following radio reports of its location. I got the cruiser up to 100mph, switched on the lights and sirens, and it was like flying. The roads were empty but for a few other cops and they just waved me on through. It was hands-down the most exhilarating experience of my life. Right then in the middle of what would later be viewed as my moment of greatest madness, I felt saner than ever, clear, clean, triumphant, alive.

"Whoa," everyone said, shaking their heads.

"Just then a news van roared past me in the other direction, the driver gesticulating wildly," Agnes said.

"Telling you look out!" Lynsie shouted.

"No doubt. Suddenly the thing dropped out of the sky right in front of me. I stomped on the gas pedal even harder and roared toward it. Then, at the moment of truth, it shifted direction, danced away from the road and went away to the east. I let off the gas and just rolled awhile. I pulled over and barely got it in park before my entire body went rigid and began shaking uncontrollably. I tell most people it was like an epileptic fit but really, truth you guys, I orgasmed. I mean kundalini lightning bolt divine ecstatic blast full body orgasm from head to toe. Never before and never again have I experienced anything like it." Agnes sighed.

"Oh my gawd," Jackie exhaled in relief.

"I had felt so dead yet simultaneously so anxious and sad for so long. Now suddenly here I was shot out of a cannon. So alive having come so close to death. Speaking of which, as it turned out, that tornado grew and grew and wound up killing everything in its path, including some three-dozen people in one town. I saw images of these home foundations swept clean and a kid's tricycle embedded in a tree.

"What happened to the cop car?" Salem asked.

"Yeah, Agnes," Jackie asked. "What didja do with the cop car?"

"Huh? Oh, nothin. I just left it there and walked home."

"Did you... get in trouble?" Lynsie asked cautiously.

Agnes shrugged. "They came and got me, but I never got charged. I guess they figured I was insane. That's when the doctors got hold of me."

Agnes stared out the window, a faraway look in her eyes.

"What do they have on you? I mean, what do they have you ON, if you don't mind me asking?" Buzz asked.

"Zoloft," Agnes replied.

Buzz nodded. "No kidding? Me too."

Lynsie squeezed Buzz's hand and added, "I've been on Paxil for two years."

Jackie stared at them in disbelief. "No way!" she exclaimed. "No way?!"

Lynsie shrugged. "I resisted for a long time, but it helped me. The meds were hard at first, but after a while, I started feeling alive again. It's like waking up."

"Until you've been there, you just don't know," Buzz added quietly.

Jackie folded her arms, clearly agitated. "Yeah, well, I'm with Holly Golightly. I say never allow yourself to get used to anything! If you do, you might as well be dead."

Agnes's expression hardened. "I was dead without the meds, Jackie."

Jackie looked to Salem for support. "Jesus, am I the only one who's sane around here? Salem? Salem?"

Salem met her gaze steadily. "You take drugs, too, Jackie."

"To get high! That's different. I don't NEED to take them!"

Salem raised his hand, cutting off the argument. "Everything's fine, come on! This is ridiculous. Let's get out of here. Let's go drink."

At that very moment yet another train roared by rattling the windows and making them all jump. In those few roaring seconds, Salem faced the severity of his lie. Why he was here and where he was going smacked him upside the head psychically. *Everything's fine?* Nothing could be further from the truth. The desperation and raw courageous action of Agnes's story had both impressed and shaken him. An all too familiar wind blew through his bones. He had been doing his best to stay drunk and high-spirited, to stay away from the sad truth of where his life had ended up.

Just then a horrible stench hit them all simultaneously and they piled out of the tiny Amtrak sleeper cabin. Everyone except Agnes made retching sounds and screeched and shouted and gasped the relatively sweet air of the corridor with its cigarette smoke and porta potty odors. The others laughed and chattered and chided Agnes as they moved toward the café car. Ruminating Salem, however, lingered several paces behind.

Like someone rapid cycling through the stages of grief, Salem realized he was now in the anger stage. Agnes' powerful story had left him awed but also angry—angry at what he saw as a world of poisoned food and greedy soulless corporate culture chemically, aesthetically, and socially whittling away at individuality and mental health. Someday all that would be left of the United States would be Agneses leaping off cliffs trading their young lives for that one ecstatic moment of clarity, sanity, truth, freedom.

Later that afternoon, Jackie and Salem sat across from each other in a cramped booth. The faint clatter of the train on the tracks underscored their conversation.

"They're not insane, Jackie," Salem said, his voice carrying the weight of certainty. "Believe me, I know. You want insane? People who live in suburbia, in prefab stucco birdcages, working jobs they hate and retiring to TV all night is insane. That my dear is INSANE."

Jackie leaned back; arms crossed. "They chose to live quiet lives and work boring jobs. So what?"

"No." Salem shook his head firmly. "I said hate. Jobs that they hate. If someone is truly content at a mundane job, great. We should all be so lucky to be easily contented. But a life shaped around fear of consequences is just plain wrong. It's insane. You stay at a job you hate because you fear the consequences of quitting? Bingo. Insane. You stay in an unhealthy relationship because you're scared of being alone? Whammo. Psycho. Given the endless alternatives in life and the imperative of living each day like it's your last, anything but the dogged pursuit of your most outrageous and wonderful dreams is—you guessed it—insane!"

Jackie sighed. "Fine. Let's change the subject."

"Okay." Salem leaned forward, his eyes sparkling with mischief. "Imagination! Why don't people use their imaginations a little? Why do most people live in stucco shoebox houses and never think of something different? Like, I don't know, an oval-shaped house with beer bottle walls and tube-slide exits for a zippy morning rush? Or a shark-shaped car with radiator teeth and factory fins? Imagination!"

Jackie smirked. "Yeah? And how often do you use your imagination? How imaginative is boxed wine?"

Salem chuckled. "Hmm. You sure enjoyed drinking my unimaginative wine, thank you. That's why we're now stuck with canned train beer at $3.50 a pop."

As if summoned, Agnes appeared at their booth with a cardboard drink carrier holding three beers.

Salem beamed. "Agnes, you're the best. And you're a psychic. We were just discussing imagination and how rarely people use theirs. I bet you use yours all the time. Probably more than people use their turn signals or their ATM cards." Salem pronounced the last few words in a kind of rap melody.

"Uh oh here comes a rap," Jackie warned Agnes.

Salem continued. "...or their Juicemaster, Stairmaster, Masters & Johnson, synthetic electric quivering dildos, and handcuffs." He laughed loudly at his own staccato delivery.

Agnes raised her beer and winked at Salem. Two men in cowboy hats in a nearby booth glanced over, their attention caught by Salem's rap.

Drawing energy from the attention, Salem spoke louder. His drunken slur vanished as his voice projected with conviction.

"Well, maybe not as much as their dildos," he continued. "What with daddy zonked out on Coors and bored flaccid by his castrated life, and his haggish wife, and his Internet porn maintenance routine and diet of young beauties in positions obscene, his daily release of twenty millennia of obsessive instinctual seed-planting big boner procreational mojo, the kind of pumped up go-getter jizm juice that gets flowing with every tight blouse, big-tit-spilling, sex-selling advert that smacks him in the face like bear mace from billboards to sitcoms to glossy lingerie catalogues reminding him again and again that his life sucks and it always will.

Two middle-aged women in an adjoining booth rose and left, disgust written on their faces. As they exited, a Black couple took their place, intrigued by Salem's rant.

By now, others in the café car had stopped their conversations, listening intently. Noticing the growing audience, Salem climbed onto the seat back, addressing the crowd.

"And speaking of things that suck and the slow, insidious castration of the spirit, what's happening to this country when you can lose an hour of your life comparison-shopping shampoo through the umpteen brands of shampoo, deodorant, breakfast cereal and prepackaged microwave meals at the local Mallmart, but, come time to vote for the leader of the Western world, you get two choices—a coin toss between two evils?"

Light applause broke out. A college student called out, "Yeah! What's up with that?"

Jackie rolled her eyes. Salem, spurred on by the audience, continued.

"Whatever happened to mom-and-pop stores and the curmudgeonly waitress at Stan's Diner and Uncle Tony's neighborhood pizzeria? Everywhere you go now it's a small world, the same world…

A 60-something gentleman in a white collared shirt and Member's Only jacket looked out the window of the train as Salem recited and saw with the ease of long life of experience and memory, a highway from the past, an Old Route 66 scene with diners and non-brand name hometown shops, everything unique unto itself.

Salem's rant continued.

"Now it's Anytown USA with all the comfy corporate mega-brands you've come to expect and that are draining the soul out of the world. Now it's an always Wal-Mart Doc Marten Starbucks Motel 6 Billion served Hollywood Video Subway world. I don't know about you but I miss the character and innocuous aesthetics of the world where a store's name was the name of the guy behind the counter, the owner, the individual, a kind of world found now only in far rural America or the heart of crowded cities, places either too tight for a Safeway Supermarket to fit, too remote for Denny's to profit, or so scary backwards and full of hicks that they'd no sooner patronize Starbucks than pour cappuccino in their carburetor."

"That would be me," a man in a cowboy hat piped up. The cowboy raised his hat as he spoke. Salem paused briefly to sip his beer, and the crowd erupted in cheers and laughter.

"It's a mixed up, sick up port wine and marshmallow mediocre Barry Barbra Madonna Manilow Milli Vanilli, sitcom, dotcom, rot in calm, shop til you drop, suck off a cop, lump in your throat, why bother vote, cubicle cage road rage minimum wage WTO media snow job corn cob up the tear gas ass wipe TV tripe clear-cuttin, tree-huggin hurtin for certain Thurston burstin packin and smackin and crackin consumption corrupted soul-abducted, two party oligarchic debtor nation under dog unconstitutional with shopping malls and suburban sprawls for all!"

Agnes with her eyes closed could see it all. The tabloid magazine celebrity faces, the characters of Married w/Children, an iMac computer, holiday shoppers fighting over a popular toy, a cop tearing up a ticket as a woman unzips his fly, footage of an office shooting spree, a drive-by shooting, a kid flipping burgers, the WTO riots on the news, a tree-sitter in a lone tree left alive surrounded by clear cut, 15-year old high school shooter Kip Kinkel killing his parents and shooting up his school in Springfield, Oregon, a crack pipe being fired up, the White House appearing in the cloud of crack smoke, and a rising shot of a shopping mall complex surrounded by endless suburban development.

The crowd erupted in applause, a burst of rebellious energy. Salem raised his beer, triumph lighting his face.

"God bless America! And God bless Amtrak! Killed by Ford and Goodyear, pared down and subsidized, losing steam to the Teamsters and the friendly skies, but still trying!"

"To Amtrak!" the crowd echoed, their voices ringing with camaraderie. Even Jackie clapped, a reluctant smile breaking through.

The train rattled onward, its passengers alive with shared defiance, their spirits lifted by Salem's unfiltered words.

Later, Salem stood in the aisle with Jackie and Agnes. Jackie popped a pill and steadied herself, her arms folded across her chest.

Agnes burped loudly, attracting the attention of people in the surrounding seats. Both Jackie and Agnes were slurring heavily.

"What now?" Jackie slurred.

"No more ranting. I promise. Now are you ready, girls?" Salem said.

"Mommy, are we there yet?" Agnes slurred back.

"You're gonna like this. This is good stuff, a free high, like kid drugs," Salem replied.

"Ooh! Like spinning around in circles! I love that!" Agnes said, and she started spinning. Given her size, her drunkenness, and the natural sway of the train, she was an immediate liability. Salem grabbed her.

"Okay. Don't do that. You're gonna need your balance for this. Now, quickly, before the sun sets and we lose all light outside," Salem instructed.

Outside, the train passed through a rural hamlet. The sun was ten minutes from setting on the horizon.

Salem moved Jackie around in front of him and pointed her up the empty aisle in the direction of the locomotive. "Okay. Agnes, listen up because you're going next. When I tell you, Jackie, start walking. Instead of watching where you're stepping, let go of your focus, pull back, and concentrate on seeing mostly peripherally out the window. Trick your mind into flying against the outside world. Ready? If you do it right, it's suddenly like you're unhinged from the train and ripping through space while standing upright. It's groovy. Now go."

Jackie began walking. Salem and Agnes followed a little behind. As her focus changed, Jackie stumbled a bit, then began walking faster and laughing as she went.

Agnes stumbled, and Salem steadied her. "Nope. I'm not doing this. I'll puke."

"Okay, Agnes. Just keep walking. I got you," Salem said. "When it comes to sobriety," Salem now exclaimed loud enough for Jackie and half the car to hear him, "..the train is a great equalizer. No one can see you stumble and accuse you of being drunk!"

A middle aged man with drink in hand blew by them in the opposite direction crashing into seated passengers as he went, now on the left, now on the right.

"The rhythmic swagger of the train makes drunks of us all!" Salem shouted with glee.

Jackie was discovering the trick of flying against the outside world.

"Haha! This is great! Whatta trip!" she exclaimed.

"Isn't it great? Simple, but it works," Salem said.

"I'm gonna barf," Agnes announced.

"No no don't barf!"

At the far end of the car, Jackie began jumping up and down and clapping. "Let's do it again!" she shouted. Salem and Agnes closed the gap between them and Jackie. Salem sat Agnes down. He resumed his instructions.

"Okay. But it's different going the other way. Maybe even more trippy. You're essentially walking against the train and with the world outside. If you perceive it correctly, it will feel like the slightest leap off the floor would suddenly affix you to the fixed space outside the train, sending you smashing against the back wall of the coach in a matter of a microsecond. You'd essentially be hit by the train from the inside, far less polite than throwing yourself in front of the train on the outside. But that's another story," Salem said.

"Huh?" Jackie and Agnes said in unison.

"Forget it. Just rambling. Go ahead," Salem replied.

Jackie proceeded down the aisle, skipping as she went. "Weeeeee!" she cried.

The instrumental opening of the song *Jockey Full of Bourbon* strummed in Salem's head as he followed Jackie down the aisle watching the outside world whiz by at an alarming rate. It was a Tom Waits song used throughout the Jim Jarmusch film Down by Law. Salem loved that song, that film, that place. He had it burned into his brain from years of repeated play. A few cars down Jackie and Salem about-faced and returned in sync with the movement of the train.

High in the sky above the train, an eagle looked down on the train with mild animal amusement, the detached but watchful eye of the hunter.

Roaring by to those on the ground, to the eagle the train merely hissed across the snowy earth, a skinny obsidian snake amidst the pink clouds now darkening to a blood orange red.

Back in the car where they'd started, they found Agnes much recovered. Salem guided her gently through the same motions. Now Jackie, Agnes, and Salem laughed and pushed each other as they ran up and down the length of the car. Outside, the train roared and spit snow spray and rattled and raged, a monster threatening to breach its cage. The world outside turned gray, then black as night fell, and the train slipped ever eastward into the dark.

Later, in the coach seats, Salem and Jackie sat together. A woman across the aisle knitted contentedly. Salem sipped a beer and wrote in his steno pad.

It's 8 p.m., and we are steadily approaching the Mt. Everest of cocked-dom. So why are Jackie and I planted in coach like two suburban stuffed monkey couch potatoes and not out haunting the bowels of Amtrak's train #1027 with our crazed rail companions? Good question.

Salem turned his attention from the window to Jackie, her head on his shoulder, eyes closed. "Jackie. Why aren't we out haunting the bowels of the snake with our hammerhead compadres?"

Jackie didn't move and spoke drunkenly, her eyes still closed. "Because we're hammered."

"Oh yeah," Salem said, turning back to the dark window and his writing.

I see phantom trees all a blur in a dark sky dappled on the glass with reflections of the lights inside the train. There is a town of some sort, the whistle of the locomotive far, far ahead like a thousand coach cars away, Christmas lights and stars, then nothing again. Such a shame that the greater scenery, like Glacier National Park and this that I imagine spectacular, passes us at night unseen. For such reasons do we drink to pass the time. On this never-ending train, nothing is in our control but the drink.

"If you could be..." Jackie began, her eyes still closed. "If you could be the sole confidante of just one person in the whole world but absolutely never tell their secrets, who would you choose?"

"Hmm. That's a tough one. You're not as drunk as you sound. I would have to say... Kurt Cobain," Salem said.

"He's dead. Disqualified," Jackie murmured.

"Yeah, well, okay. Thanks for explaining the rules. Kurt could have used me as a friend. A confidante. Somebody other than that nasty predatorial wife of his. If he'd had me in his corner, he might be alive and thus qualify. Layne Staley, then. Who would you pick?" Salem asked.

"Madonna," Jackie blurted. "Hands down."

"Oh-ho!" Salem laughed.

Buzz and Lynsie walked down the aisle into view. Buzz had his arm around Lynsie, and they appeared sloppy smitten with one another. "Hey, Salem. Jackie sleeping?" Buzz asked.

Jackie opened her eyes and sat up. "I was molting, thank you. Now, thanks to you people, my feathers will never come in."

"Soooo... where have you two been all even-innnggg?" Salem inquired, dragging the last syllable like a creepy butler at a castle door.

Buzz replied, "Well, sure enough, somebody claimed that room right after we all cleared out. Lynsie and I lingered a while in the hall, and wouldn't you know, another room opened. The steward was nowhere to be seen, never even came to change the sheets. So..."

Lynsie piped up excitedly, "We made love on somebody's dirty sheets!"

"Eeewww!" Jackie said.

"Sounds sweet to me," Salem shrugged.

Jackie reached into her purse, pulled out a compact, opened it to reveal a nest of red pills, and popped one in her mouth. "I gotta pee," she said, rising and taking her leave of the gang.

"Well, Salem, we're heading back to Lynsie's car. She's getting off tomorrow morning, and I guess we're all pretty much blowing to the four winds in Chicago, eh? So, if you wanna have a kind of farewell party tonight, come grab us, and we'll hit the cafe car," Buzz said.

"Yeah, yeah, Buzz. Okay. See ya later," Salem replied.

Lynsie and Buzz sauntered off, Lynsie skipping like a schoolgirl. Salem looked across the aisle at a pair of old people sleeping sitting up, her head on his shoulder as they swayed with the sideways motion of the train.

"Another of God's cruel jokes, like dog-ugly faces on hot bodies and goddesses with bad gas. God lets old people sleep sitting up. What a crime. What bliss. The frogs I would kiss. If only I could sleep like that," he muttered aloud.

An idea struck Salem. He reached into his jacket for the bottle of pills. "Eenie, meenie, mynie, moe. Down the hatch!" Slumping low, he washed down the pill with the last of a now warm beer, took pen in hand and took to his steno pad.

People who fly and complain of jet lag are cowards. Ride cross-country on a train hardly sleeping for three days, and you'll experience a true physical and temporal lag like none other. Time becomes one long strange mélange of yesterday and today, today and tomorrow. A day without end, a night...

Shadowy figures of industry and houses flashed by in the pitch-black night outside Salem's window. Without a moon and given the reflected light from inside the coach car, it was difficult to see out at all.

...a night that lasts forever. A night of crazed rambling clickity-clack thoughts and oddities from the subconscious cellar of the stupefied, insomniac mind. Anything can happen.

Salem opened his eyes and saw Agnes leaning over him.

"How's the weather in Neverland?" Agnes asked.

"Huh? Oh, I wasn't sleeping. I never sleep," Salem replied.

"Uh-huh. You were mumbling some strange shit."

"Did I say something about Neverland?" he asked.

Agnes took Jackie's seat and leaned in closer. "Maybe. You were moaning mostly. Sounded nice," she said, her tone turning playful.

"Where's Eric?" Salem asked.

"Probably pouting in a toilet somewhere. He's not speaking to me right now because I called him by your name accidentally. Forget him. It's only nine o'clock, and I know a warrior like you doesn't need sleep. It's our last night."

Agnes revealed two airplane bottles of tequila she had hidden behind her back.

"Here. We'll knock these back and get going. We have a mission. We must derail this train with our drunken debauchery before the sunrise scatters us to the four winds!" she exclaimed with mock drama.

Salem smiled and fought off tears. One escaped and rolled down the cheek facing Agnes. She leaned in and kissed it gently.

"You know, you haven't farted in like, hours," Salem said with a smirk.

"Yeah, so? What did you think I was the sister who farts herself to death in *Like Water for Chocolate*?"

"HA! I dunno. Maybe," he teased.

Agnes raised an eyebrow. "I bet you've never farted before, huh?"

"Never!! No, I'm guilty. I hate my own farts. I hate having to go to the bathroom. I hate having ear wax. I'm hate the sticky mess of the male orgasm. If I had my way, I'd be a cyborg, maybe a locomotive. Machines I understand. But the human body, oof. Too messy."

Agnes cracked the bottles open and handed one to Salem. "To our imperfect, oozing stinking slobbering selves! God's finest creation!"

"To oozing," Salem agreed.

They toasted and drank to the dregs.

"My best friend's name is Bitchface." Agnes said matter-of-factly.

Salem raised his eyebrows in surprise.

"This is her favorite tequila," she said.

"To Bitchface!" Salem replied, raising his bottle.

Late that night, the sound of Agnes cackling and Salem singing echoed down the stairwell from above as they descended to the lower level. Salem, imitating the raspy voice of Tom Waits, belted out lyrics with drunken flair.

"That's where old George found himself out there at the crossroads," he sang. "You think you can take them bullets and leave 'em, do you? Just save a few for your bad days. Well... pretty soon all your days are bad without the bullets. Kid, you're hooked. Heavy as lead."

Agnes threw an arm around Salem as they stumbled toward the bathrooms, fresh from one last party with friends in the café car.

"You... are... insane," Agnes slurred heavily.

"Why thank you," Salem said with a bow. "Do you like my Tom Waits impression?"

"I do. And now I must pee before I pee on you," Agnes declared, darting for the bathroom.

"Wait! Come back. That could be fun," Salem called after her with a laugh.

He turned to the exit door window, opened it, and stuck his head out. The train moved at a moderate speed. The sound of the horn sifted and shifted through the howling wind now close, now far ahead and faint. It was the lonely call of the outcast wolf.

The train rounded a corner, revealing the chain of locomotives ahead. The headlights illuminated haystacks, the occasional cow, a farmhouse in the distance. A warning sign on the door read:

OPENING WINDOW STRICTLY PROHIBITED!

As a signal pole whipped by, Salem jerked his head back inside. "Whew! That was close," he muttered, looking down and noticing an unexpected bulge in his jeans. Surprised, he was tapping at it just as Agnes returned.

"Hmm? Whatcha got there? Well, I'm happy to see you, too," Agnes teased.

Salem forced a smile and laughed nervously.

Agnes grabbed Salem by a belt loop just above his crotch. "Come. Let Aggie help you out with that," she said, leading him to a bathroom. Once inside, she locked the door, unbuttoned his pants and leaned into him. Salem watched as Agnes squatted and disappeared in the bathroom mirror.

"Agnes. Oh, Agnes. This can't be good for your re.. LAY.. shun.. Ship," Salem said stutteringly, his voice rising an octave. Agnes raised a hand like a student with a question, but Salem guessed no words would be coming from her mouth for a while. She touched a shushing finger to his lips.

"Oh dear," he murmured to himself now as Agnes was quite busy and the ambient decibel level in the metallic bathrooms was twice that of the carpeted coach. "This is the slipping of the gears, the loose and chipped-tooth meandering between first and third-degree infidelity, between good and the so-called evil existent in the animal man, in us all, if only more pronounced in the boxed-wine hearts of men..." Salem paused and glanced down at Agnes. "And women for whom chaos is a familiar friend."

Later the bathroom door creaked open, and Agnes stumbled out. Her left breast had escaped her low-cut blouse, and she replaced it, swaying slightly with movement of the train. She walked down the hall and disappeared up the stairwell.

Inside the bathroom, Salem sat on the toilet, his head in his hands. The motion of the train caused him to rock side to side.

"Agnes. Mmmm. Agnes, Agnes, Agnes. Who would have thought... Aaaaaaaag-nesssssssssss," he sung to the tune of Toto's *Rosanna*.

His head slumped forward as he drifted in post-orgasmic reverie, the rhythmic clatter of the train singing him rapidly to sleep.

* * *

Up in the engine room of the lead locomotive, an eerie calm threatened amidst the thrum of diesel engines and hum of related machinery. Something was wrong. The engineer sat slumped in his chair, fast asleep, his posture impossibly straight. At that moment, no one was driving the train. Engineer seats are designed to make falling asleep impossible. A trigger in the seat is designed to release when the engineer falls out of it, stopping the train.

Red signals flashed by the windows, unnoticed by the unconscious engineer. Then, in the distance, a pair of headlights appeared, growing larger and brighter with every passing second.

Suddenly, the blare of another train's horn cut through the night, jarring the engineer awake. His face twisted in horror as the oncoming locomotive filled the windshield. It was too late. The engine room disintegrated upon impact.

The fiery collision sent shockwaves through the train. Five locomotive engines devoured each other in a domino effect catastrophic head-on crash. Coach cars crumpled and folded like paper boxes, the explosions lighting up the night as though the sun had risen early for a brief, terrible moment.

Salem jolted awake in the train bathroom, screaming. His chest heaved as he tried to shake off the vivid nightmare.

A short time later, Salem stood at the open exit door window to the lower-level, the wind tearing through his hair and wiping his thoughts clean. The train, safe as houses, rattled on carrying him and several hundred other souls safely through the dark. As night gave way to dawn, Salem remained at the door, window open, a cigarette trembling in his hand. His face was haggard, haunted by sleeplessness and the ghosts of his own mind.

The same large sign on the door beside him stood by, ignored:

LOSING ONE'S HEAD STRICTLY PROHIBITED!

The distant sound of a two-way radio crackled through the air, accompanied by the footfalls of a conductor descending the stairs. Recognizing the sounds, Salem snapped out of his doldrums, quickly flicked his cigarette into the wind, closed the window, and resumed staring out of it.

"Is that you smoking down here?" a woman's voice called out.

"Nope," Salem replied without turning.

"You know the smoking room is in the next car. May I see your ticket?"

"Fucking authorities," Salem mumbled under his breath. *Give a man a hammer..*

Reaching into his breast pocket, Salem thrust his ticket and an I.D. at the conductor without looking back.

"A reporter? Very well then. If there's anything I can do for you, just ask for Helen okay?"

Salem froze. His face went pale as a chill ran through him. The name echoed in his mind, triggering a memory he thought well-buried.

"Do you wanna get laid?"

"What?!!" In the reflection in the glass, Salem saw a scene from long ago, Helen his much older boss peering down at him where he lay drugged, unable to move, her eyes hungry as she rode him to climax. Salem staggered, clutching the wall for support as the flashback ended.

"I said are you okay? Do you want to lie down?" the conductor asked, concern in her voice.

Salem blinked, his vision swimming as he turned to face the woman. Relief flooded him when he saw the conductor's youthful face and black hair. This Helen was far too young to be the one from his past.

"Holy fuck," Salem muttered, his voice barely above a whisper.

A short time later, Salem appeared in the glass behind a door. The door slid open, and Salem hurriedly walked down the aisle to his seat. Neither Jackie, Agnes, nor Buzz were anywhere to be seen.

"Shit!" he muttered, quickening his pace.

He passed through another car, two more sets of doors, and descended the stairs to the café. He looked around. They weren't there. The snack bar steward shot him a curious look.

Salem mounted the stairs and ran back the way he came, past his seat, and down another set of stairs to his car's bathroom area. The exit area was empty.

"Shit!" Salem cursed again.

He opened the window just as the train came to a complete stop. Sticking his head out, he scanned the platform. Several cars down, Lynsie and Buzz stepped off. Buzz was carrying Lynsie's bag. Jackie followed behind them.

"Hey! Hey, Buzz!" Salem shouted, but his voice went unheard over the noise of the train.

Frustrated, he slammed the window shut. His hand moved to the door latch, hesitating for a moment.

I had always wanted to open one of these doors, Salem thought. *Preferably at 70 miles an hour with a freight train passing in the other direction in a mad, screaming steel Technicolor blur just inches away, but this would have to do.*

With a determined motion, Salem undid a lock hasp with one hand and cranked a big lever with the other thus opening the door. He leaped out and ran down the platform.

"Well, if it isn't Mr. Disappear in the Night!" Jackie called out with a smirk.

"Hey, Salem! Glad you could make it," Buzz added.

"Hi, Salem," Lynsie said softly.

Salem leaned down to hug the petite Lynsie. "Hey, Lynsie. I just remembered a few minutes ago that this was your stop. But where are you guys going?"

"They said over the train's P.A. that we'd be delayed here for an hour," Buzz replied.

"We thought we'd see Lynsie off in style," Jackie explained. "She said she knows of a place nearby that makes great Bloody Marys."

"Now that's the best news I've heard all morning," Salem said, grinning. Then his expression shifted. "Hey, anybody seen Agnes?"

Everyone shrugged and shook their heads.

"Hmm. She must've gotten off last night. She and Eric, I mean," Salem said thoughtfully.

Jackie shot him a suspicious glance. "Uh-huh," she said, "I bet she did."

Al & Vic's Tavern was a relic of another era, a narrow watering hole that no doubt dated to the end of Prohibition. It had a bar trimmed in teak with a dozen red vinyl stools lining the counter and half a dozen tables scattered throughout. Dust coated the overwhelming array of knickknacks and decorations. Two very old men tended the bar, moving at a deliberate almost slo-motion pace.

Giant jars of pickled pig's feet and pickled eggs sat on the counter. A sign on the wall read:

GIZZARDS FOR SALE, $5 A POUND, $3 A HALF POUND

Jackie, Salem, Lynsie, and Buzz sat along the bar. Beside them, an old couple argued at a table.

"I'm telling you the truth, Baby. You know I wouldn't lie to you, Baby," the drunk man slurred.

"Is that so? God, you're a piece of work. Bartender, another whiskey," the drunk woman shot back.

"What about me, Baby?" he asked.

"What about *you*?" she replied coldly. "Git your own!"

"Okay, Baby. You win. Old Gravy's just a turpentined turd. Let's go home and have grudge sex, baby, come on."

Jackie, Salem, Lynsie, and Buzz exchanged amused glances.

"I've decided to detrain here," Buzz announced. "Spend Christmas with Lynsie."

"No shit! Well, all right, Buzz. Got yourself an American woman," Salem said with a grin.

"You go, girl," Jackie added.

Lynsie smiled. "I guess that leaves just you two."

"Yep. You're stuck with little ole me all the way to Boston," Jackie teased, elbowing Salem affectionately.

Salem pursed his lips and raised his eyebrows.

Jackie laughed and reached for her drink as Salem pulled out a stash of pills. He poured out six blue capsules, slid three to Jackie, and swallowed the others.

"Here's to the sole survivors. Um, you might wanna eat just one of those now and save the others. Eat them all now and I might have to carry you back to the train," Salem warned.

"What about you? You just ate three!" Jackie exclaimed.

"Yeah, I did, didn't I?" Salem replied nonchalantly.

Jackie eyed the bartender warily before popping one capsule. Salem glanced nervously at the two pills left on the counter.

"Honestly, I thought these were something else," he admitted.

"What are they?" Jackie asked.

"Demeral. It's a little like heroin. Strong."

Jackie grinned. "Ooh-wee. Here we go!"

By 8:30, the drinks were drained, and the group's energy had shifted. Jackie stretched and stood. "Um, I hate to break it up, kids, but we should be heading back. Love to spend the holidays with you, Lynsie, but..."

Salem, chewing on a pickled green bean from his drink, made loud sucking sounds with his straw as he tried to drain the last drop from his glass. It appeared that if he could have fit his head in the glass, he would have.

"Man, those were good bloodies," he slurred.

Jackie, though clearly high, managed to keep her composure better than Salem.

"Oh, shit," she muttered as the four stood and ambled toward the exit.

"Thanks, Al! Thanks, Vic!" Jackie and Lynsie called out in unison.

The two old bartenders turned and waved. "Thank you, kids! Merry Christmas!"

"Dynamite bloodies. You guys rock!" Salem added as he staggered out the door.

Al gave a thumbs-up as the group exited.

On the sidewalk, Jackie, Lynsie, Buzz, and Salem stood awkwardly. Salem leaned heavily on Jackie. Buzz pulled himself away from Lynsie just long enough for everyone to say goodbye.

"Buzz, hold him, will ya?" Jackie said with a laugh. "Bye, Lynsie. It was nice getting to know ya."

Buzz supported Salem while Jackie and Lynsie embraced.

"Bye, Jackie," Lynsie said softly.

"Bye, you guys. It's been beautiful! Goodbye, sweet Lynsie. Thank you for putting up with a bunch of drunk crazies," Salem said, slurring as he waved.

"Hey! Don't leave me out of that," Lynsie replied with a grin.

"All right, you drunk crazy. Don't break Buzz's heart," Salem said with a wink.

"Take care of him!" Buzz called as Jackie helped Salem across the street.

"I'll try!" Jackie replied.

The pair approached a liquor store. Jackie's eyes lit up. "Ooh! Supplies!"

Salem chuckled as they entered the store together.

Jackie exited the liquor store holding a jug of wine in one hand and a swaggering Salem in the other. They rounded a corner, and the train came into view.

"Wait! I want clove cigarettes. I gotta go back," Jackie said, stopping abruptly.

Salem looked warily at the train. "What about the train? We might miss the train."

"Can you stand right here with the wine? Promise not to go anywhere? I'll be right back," Jackie said, placing the wine at Salem's feet before running back toward the store.

Oblivious, Salem swaggered off toward the train. Approaching it from the front, he noticed the engineer was not in his seat, and there were still people standing outside the doors smoking.

"Phew! That was close! Jackie?" Salem called, glancing over his shoulder. Suddenly the world telescoped out before him. The liquor store was now miles away, Al & Vic's an eternity. And Jackie? Had she ever existed? Salem couldn't say. He returned his attention to the giant, idling engine before him. Perhaps by virtue of its thundering noisy presence, it was where it was supposed to be.

Checking to ensure no one was watching, he stepped off the platform onto the tracks directly in front of the engine. The step was bigger than he expected, and he nearly fell.

Regaining his balance, Salem assumed an authoritative stance, holding out an arm as if commanding the train to halt. He laughed to himself but abruptly stopped, his expression shifting to a frown. A sudden chill ran through him, and he quickly stumbled back onto the platform.

As he started to pass the front of the engine to walk down alongside it, something in the corner of his vision stopped him cold.

The blood drained from his face.

Salem turned slowly. Standing there, smoking a cigarette and staring directly at him, was the woman in the blue dress—the same woman whose suicide he had witnessed a decade before.

Suddenly the Earth rushed up to meet Salem as he lost consciousness and face planted onto the platform beside the lead locomotive.

THE BEGINNING

Money's just something you throw off the back of a train. Got a head full of lightning, a hat full of rain. I love you pretty baby but I always take the long way home.

TOM WAITS

Salem's eyes fluttered open, the world around him slowly coming into focus. As the haze cleared, a black-and-white photo of a young Amelia Earhart filled his vision, so close it felt like it was being thrust into his face.

He rubbed his eyes and sat sprawled on a massive, throne-like curved oak bench, an elegant relic in Boston's South Station. Suspended from the ceiling four stories above was a massive portrait of Earhart, alongside similar images of Einstein and Edison, emblazoned with the words:

Think different.

"Think different. Huh. Lotta good that's done me," Salem muttered. He glanced around at the bustling station, a quizzical expression on his face.

Where am I? he thought. *I have no idea.*

Salem had no recollection of getting to wherever he was. As he thought about it longer, he had no memory of anything since Agnes and the bathroom. Still lying down, Salem reached out and grabbed the shirtsleeve of a man rolling by in a wheelchair.

"Excuse me. Can you tell me, uh... where I am?"

The man stopped, gave him a hard look, and barked a laugh. "You're kidding? You able-bodied people make me laugh. Especially a dink like you who don't know how lucky you are 'cuz you're too damn busy trying to kill yourself. What was it? Acid? Shrooms? Night Train? An old bottle of quaaludes?"

Salem sat up, adjusted his sunglasses, and mumbled, "Meperidine. For pain. Doctor's orders."

"Pain! You don't know dick about pain," the man shot back.

"Look, I didn't ask you to role-play my father. I just—"

"Fine!" the man snapped, wheeling himself away. As he moved, he shouted back over his shoulder.

"Boston! USA! Earth! Finest fucking clams in the Universe! Ahahaha! And here they come now!"

Just then, a tide of commuters, predominantly women in office attire, warm jackets, and sneakers, poured into the station from an arriving train. Salem sat dumbfounded as they sped past him.

Salem watched the tide come and go, his focus eventually shifting to the towering portrait of Amelia Earhart.

My God. Look at them. Where are they going? Granted, I didn't exactly know where I was going, but I was pretty sure I'd had fun getting here. Had they had fun? he mused. *Waking up to an alarm clock in the dark for twenty years, answering to people they hated all day, returning home in the dark half the year, ingesting corporate messages to think for themselves when in fact the corporations wanted nothing of the kind from them. And in the end, watering down their dreams repeatedly until there was nothing left but water—the water of puddles, the water of toilets, the water of tears.*

In his mind's eye he rose higher, taking in the vastness of

the station, the sea of humanity rushing about below him. The enormous oak bench where he sat grew smaller and smaller amidst the crowd as his thoughts soared.

Suddenly being me doesn't seem so bad. Suddenly I'm almost giddy as I peer skyward and interpret Amelia's message as written directly to me, an affirmation of my every breath scrawled across the station sky. Sometimes you just forget, like the guy in the wheelchair said. When you've lived like I have, always on the fringe, the edge, the outer limits, you forget sometimes that it's okay to be different because your whole life is such an exaggeration, such a Mad Hatter morph on the word different, and all the messages coming in from the so-called real world chant freak, uncool, wrong, aberration. Enough of that and pretty soon you either surrender to their side, you learn to tune it out, or you freak out and want to die.

Snow fell outside, blanketing the gray Boston morning in dense, swirling flakes. The scene continued to rise, carrying Salem's thoughts higher, into the cold sky.

Later that day, Salem sat by the window on a southbound train, his notebook open on his lap, occasionally scribbling notes. The train cut through grim, gray weather, snow falling steadily outside the window. Beside him, a stout man in his mid-30s with a thick Boston accent gesticulated wildly as he regaled Salem with stories from his life.

"...So, we finish the project, and it's a real big to-do," Bob began. "I'm the foreman on the thing, so the whole thing rests on my shoulders, right? So, all the big wigs and my boss and I pile into the chopper and go for a test run and thwack! Wouldn't you know it? The damn thing's not been built to spec. The chopper gets hung up on a cable, snaps the cable, towers start falling..."

I was straining to remember something about yesterday, Salem thought. *I had remembered the Demerol by now. Demon Demerol. But where had I lost Jackie? Had she deposited me on the bench in South*

Station? I just couldn't remember. Chances were good I never would.

Bob continued, "...Anyway, the chopper pilot barely got us outa there alive, but as soon as we land, bamm! I'm fired."

Fired. Salem mused. *It had an almost erotic ring to it. I'd never been fired from a job. Suddenly I wanted to run right out and get one just so I could then get fired.*

"But heh! I'm a hearty New Englandah, bro. I don't give up easy," Bob said with a grin. "I do a little searching and come up with proof that it was the client's fault, not mine. Then the shit really hit the fan. My company sues the client, wins megabucks, and I got my job back!"

Outside, the train paralleled a major freeway choked with traffic. Through the falling snow, a giant sign atop a factory announced *GILLETTE WORLD SHAVING HEADQUARTERS*. A passing truck bore a sign that read *G.O.D.*, translated below as *GUARANTEED OVERNIGHT DELIVERY*. Salem chuckled and shook his head when he saw it.

"I like you, Salem," Bob said. "Anybody who would ride a train for three and a half days to go where flying would get you in six hours has gotta be half crazy, and I like that. And you've been writing the whole time?"

Bob leaned in, trying to decipher Salem's handwriting.

"Well, I partied a bit," Salem admitted.

"Fack! That's some crazy handwriting! And you can read that?"

"I can."

"Is that shorthand?"

"No. It's my own invention, Bob. It's an illegible combination of wine-pressed vowels and codeine-numbed consonants."

Bob blinked at him, then burst out laughing. "You're a faacking riot!"

"Thanks," Salem replied with a small smile.

Salem blinked and Bob the builder was gone. Or so it seemed with train travel. On and off. Salem raised his nose and realized he could still smell Bob's aftershave. With Bob gone the seat beside Salem was empty. Salem resumed writing in his steno pad.

Just like that. Before he detrained Bob related one of the more gonzo tales of drunken, spirited revelry I'd ever heard. It seems he and his buddies stole the goalpost after their team's victory and paraded it through the streets, straight into a high-tension power line, electrocuting them all. I wasn't sure if that was funny or not, but I admired his embrace of chaos, just as he admired mine. Rail excursions are like that, allowing instant intimacy with strangers, then snatching them away with equal velocity.

The scenery outside turned post-apocalyptic. Dozens of boarded-up warehouses passed by, their windows shattered or covered with plywood. Steam billowed from smokestacks into the cold air. Rusted metal refuse littered the landscape. The hulking remains of a garbage truck leaned into the earth, its cab missing like the head of an elephant slaughtered for its ivory. The weather was grim and gray, snow swirling in thick flurries. Salem watched in silence, the grim tableau matching his mood.

As the train pulled to a stop, Salem peered nervously out the window. The platform was packed with people waiting to board, their shapes blurry in the gray snowfall. Suddenly he was panic stricken, terrified of the hairy-backed beast he felt sure would nab the empty seat beside me.

Think quick! Should I feign sleep? Puke? Fart? Remove my shoes and socks, setting them out to air beside me? Oh, you whimsical prankster Loki, mischievous god of my Viking ancestry! I just know you're going to send me a hairy dwarf!

Salem sat braced for the worst as passengers filled the seats around him. Overhead, the dull lighting reflected his growing dread.

A lovely young mother, hippyish and in her mid-20s, cradling a baby, sat down next to him. The baby took one look at Salem and began to cry. She rocked him gently, but the wails continued unabated.

Salem turned his face tight to the window, his arm shielding him from the sound, his expression cringing. Reaching into his pocket, he pulled out a lone blue capsule, raised it to his mouth, and—

The crying stopped.

Curious, Salem peeked over at the baby and his mother.

The woman had begun breastfeeding. As Salem watched, a wet spot formed on her blouse over the unoccupied breast. She turned and caught him looking but rather than frown or scold him she smiled warmly.

Embarrassed, Salem quickly stashed the uneaten pill.

"I'm so sorry," she said, her voice kind. "He's normally so well behaved. We're probably the last people you wanted sitting next to you, huh?"

"Yeah, I mean NO! It's fine. Really. I love babies," Salem replied, his voice rising slightly in protest.

She chuckled. "I'm Miyanna. Think cavewoman. Me, Anna! And this little guy... is Salem."

In that moment, the whole scene before his eyes blurred, jittered and wiggled. Had it been the train or his brain, he couldn't say. Salem shook his head to realign his vision.

"What? What did you say?"

"Salem," she repeated. You know like the town north of here. Salem witches? All that."

Salem stared in awe.

"No way."

"No, really that's his name. What's yours?"

"Salem," he stammered.

Miyanna frowned slightly. "What?"

"That's my name! Salem is my name, too."

Her expression softened into a curious smile. "Wow. I knew there was something about you. I felt it the moment I looked at you."

"You did?" Salem asked, his voice quieter.

"I did," she said, her smile warm and unhurried. Cradling the baby, she extended a finger toward him.

Salem noticed it was her ring finger, noticeably bare. He reached out and shook it lightly.

"Hi, Big Salem," she said playfully.

As Miyanna returned her attention to the baby, Salem's gaze lingered. Slowly, she began to glow with a warm, ethereal light, like summer sun shimmering through water. Stunned, Salem threw his head back and smiled, giddy at the divine glow enveloping her and the baby.

Wow. Miyanna. A goddess. A mother! Salem thought. *Suddenly, I forgot where I was headed, and I didn't give a rat's ass about recalling the events of my day lost to demon Demerol. Suddenly, there was just Miyanna and Salem and me.*

The glow spread, engulfing Salem. Miyanna glanced at him and smiled, her radiance filling the space between them.

Salem leaned into the window and wrote verse in his head.

There is no America, no United Corporations thereof. There is no Amtrak, no train, no death, no fear of growing up or growing old. There is no forever, and no never-never. If this is a dream, I should wish to never awaken again. I could get used to this.

Outside, the train's dark and stoic face cut through the blowing snow, its progress steady and unyielding. The ashen sky mirrored the somber landscape below. Had anyone been looking while the engine passed, they couldn't have missed the single window in Salem's car glowing with a warm, orange light. A magic amber light. Among the many dark windows, it stood out like a heartbeat in a desolate winter battlefield.

The baby, Little Salem, slept peacefully in Miyanna's lap.

"...and your brother Pierre is an airline steward," Miyanna said, her voice soft.

"That's right," Salem replied with a small smile.

"A real globe-trotting family. So, what does your girlfriend think of you wandering the Earth on trains?"

"No girlfriend. No wife," Salem said, shrugging. "And what about you? You, uh, on your way to meet up with Salem's daddy in New York or something?"

Miyanna shook her head. "No. We're going to Connecticut. Salem's daddy passed."

Salem stiffened. "Oh, Jesus! I'm so sorry."

"Yeah. Well, I'm sorry that Salem won't have a father. Other than that,..." She trailed off, her tone heavy with implication.

"Yikes," Salem muttered.

"He was a bad man," she said simply.

"The dad, was he... was his name—"

"Salem? No. I named the baby."

Salem hesitated. "It's a rare name. How did you—"

"It came to me in a dream a long time ago. Hmm," she said, her voice trailing off.

Salem shifted in his seat and touched her shoulder gently. "No, please. Please tell me."

She hesitated. "Well, it's just that, well it's gonna sound crazy."

"Yes?"

"I was... I was riding a train... in the dream."

Miyanna's voice softened as she continued. "In the dream, I was going somewhere special. I don't remember where. But I was happy. Really happy."

"Go on."

"It was a brilliant, beautiful sunny day. Outside my window, there were miles and miles of pure white sand dunes in a long, narrow strip of land, beyond which a super blue sea stretched forever. The sand dunes were out the other side window as well. It was as if the train were sailing on the sand. Anyway, suddenly I just knew I had arrived. I looked out the window again, and we were stopped. I reached for my suitcase, but it was gone. In its place was a package elegantly wrapped in silver and gold foil paper."

Miyanna smiled, seeing the sugar sand dunes and ocean glide by in her mind. Her hand rested on a package on the seat beside her, wrapped in gleaming silver and gold paper.

"I took the package and stepped off the train into the sand. My feet were bare. I climbed a dune, sat down with the package in my lap, and smiled out at the sea."

"When it got dark, I lay down and slept. Oh! If I could only describe that sleep. It was the most sensual sleep I've never had. Dream sleep. Amazing.

"In the morning, I awoke to the warmth of the sun on my naked skin. Now my clothes were gone, too! But the package remained. At last, I opened it, and what do you think was inside? The name Salem. Just like that. It was just the word, just floating there like smoke.

Salem sat still, his head tilted toward Miyanna, eyes closed. Her words hung in the air.

"That's it," Miyanna said, her voice a soft sigh. "That's how Salem got his name."

Salem smiled, opening his eyes. "That's the most beautiful thing I've ever heard."

Miyanna smiled back. "How did you get the name Salem?"

"I was born there. Salem, Massachusetts."

"Oh."

Little Salem stirred, waking up with a quiet coo. Salem reached out, his hand hovering near the baby's head.

"May I?" he asked.

Miyanna's face lit up. "Yes!"

She handed him the baby. Salem cradled the small bundle, grinning so hard his face hurt. The baby smiled back.

"Hello there, little buddy! My name is Salem, too. Gosh, he's beautiful."

Miyanna tilted her head, watching the scene with obvious pleasure.

"Tomorrow is Christmas, Salem. Are you going to be with family?"

Salem handed the baby back, the joy in his eyes replaced by a flicker of anxiety. Miyanna caught the change.

"I'm sorry. It's none of my business," she said quickly.

Salem shook his head. "No. It's okay. I'm not well, Miyanna. And you... you're radiant, so fresh and young and alive. I can't... you, I mean..."

She reached out and touched a finger to his lips. "Ssshhhh. It's all right. You don't have to explain."

Salem turned to the window, his face drawn and tired once more. "I'm not going home for Christmas. I don't have a home. But I do have something that I have to take care of, something I have to finish."

Miyanna hesitated. "Salem, I want you to come home with us. Whatever it is, it can wait. Christmas is a time to be with family, with... loved ones. Salem?"

Tears streamed down Salem's face. He looked at her, trying to speak but unable to find the words.

"Salem? Whatever it..."

He turned suddenly, his face etched with pain. "NO! It can't wait! You don't understand. It can't wait."

Little Salem began to cry, startled by the outburst. Miyanna quickly soothed him, offering a nipple as she leaned closer to comfort Big Salem.

"I'm sorry," Salem said, his voice breaking. "Something terrible happened ten years ago on Christmas Day. I was there. God, all I want to do is go home, but I can't. I have to go back. I have to..."

Miyanna turned his face to hers and kissed him, softly at first, then with growing intensity. Salem felt his whole body and spirit leap and vibrate then quiver in wave upon wave of joyful surrender.

Later, Salem, Miyanna, and the baby slept together, leaned into one another as the train rumbled on. A sudden jolt snapped Salem awake. He blinked groggily, then smiled a rueful smile as he remembered where he was and with whom.

The train was approaching a station. Darkness was falling outside. Salem peered through the window, the snow whipping past. He froze, his breath catching in his throat.

There, through the swirling snow, stood a woman in light blue, staring back at him.

His heart pounded in his ears. He turned away from the window, his face pale.

"Miyanna. Wake up."

She stirred, her eyes searching his. "You're going, aren't you?"

"Yes. I have to go now."

Miyanna embraced him, her grip firm but tender. Salem pulled away, stepping into the aisle. He grabbed his bag and looked back one last time.

Miyanna wept as she spoke.

"My dream. It was you, Salem, all along. I know it now. I... gave him your name. I wasn't sure you existed. I'm glad you exist, Salem."

Too choked with emotion to respond, Salem bowed his head in acknowledgement, turned and walked down the aisle, disappearing into the snow outside.

From the window, Miyanna watched Salem cross the platform and vanish into the storm. The conductor called, "All aboard!" He retrieved the yellow footstool, closed the door, and the train began to pull away.

Miyanna held Baby Salem up to the window, straining to catch one last glimpse of him, but the snow had swallowed him whole.

* * *

The cab pulled up to the small, weathered motel, its tires crunching softly against the snow-dusted gravel. Salem stepped out into the frigid night, pulling his bag from the backseat before shutting the door. His breath clouded the air as he took in the barren winter landscape, a desolate stretch of stillness broken only by the distant sound of the wind.

Inside the motel lobby, the atmosphere was tired but cozy, the air warm. Yard sale paintings of covered bridges, farmhouses, and cows adorned the walls, their faded colors adding to the aged ambiance of the room. A dusty plastic palm tree stood forlorn in a corner near the door.

An old man appeared at the counter, his face lined with the years and an air of practiced hospitality.

"Heck of a night to be out traveling," the old man remarked, his voice cheery, musical.

"Yeah. Single room, please. Cash," Salem replied, his tone clipped but not unkind.

"Not expecting anyone else? That's a shame, Christmas Eve and all." The old man took the hundred-dollar bill and ID that Salem handed over, scrutinizing them with a practiced eye. "New Mexico? My, you really are a long way from home."

"Someplace around here I can get a drink?" Salem asked, ignoring the man's attempt at conversation.

The old man sized him up, then leaned forward conspiratorially, his voice dropping to a near whisper. "It'd be an awful shame for a nice young man like you to be alone on Christmas Eve. This old gal from my bingo group, she has a couple of young ladies that do... odd jobs for her. Real lookers. I could call her up. Be real discreet."

Salem's gaze fixed on the old man, impassive. "No. Thank you, though. Bar?"

The old man shrugged. "Suit ya-self. Killingworth Tavern. Out of the door of your room, left, one block down, left again. Can't miss it. You're in room 27. Welcome to Killingworth."

Salem turned to leave but paused at the door, his face a blank slate. Then, fighting himself, he turned back. "How much for, uh..."

The old man's eyes gleamed. "The change from your hundred would be a good start."

"Great. Well, um… Merry Christmas, then."

"Uh!" The old man gestured for the money. Salem walked back, opened his hand, and let the bills fall into the old man's grasp.

"I'll have her meet you at the bar," the old man said, grinning.

The Killingworth Tavern was a curious mix of taxidermy shop, nautical captain's quarters and bottled spirits, its homey, dark interior strangely comforting. Salem stepped inside, a tired smile creeping across his face as he took in the decor.

The tavern was conspicuously empty. Even the bartender was largely absent, leaving only Jimmy Stewart's black-and-white visage flickering on the TV. Salem settled at the bar, nursing a pint of stout as he watched Stewart's anguished journey through the streets of Potterville.

Half an hour later, Salem's head rested on his folded hands atop his empty glass. He stared at the TV as he wondered what had become of the barkeep. His eyelids grew heavy, closed and opened and closed again. From behind him, a voice startled him awake.

"Every year, I look forward to Christmas just so I can see this movie."

Salem turned to see a woman standing there. She was attractive, in her early twenties, with an easy confidence.

"Why don't you just buy the video?" Salem asked.

She smiled. "It's only magic at Christmas."

Back in room 27, Salem lay on the bed, clad only in black thermal long underwear. Beside him lay Danielle in a red silk slip, tracing lazy shapes on his bare stomach with her fingers.

"What would you like first for Christmas?" she asked softly. "Think of my body as an advent calendar and pick a door to open."

Salem eyed Danielle with a look of surprise and nodded in admiration. "What's a Brown educated girl like you doing with a guy like me on this most familial night of the year?"

"Maybe I followed a star here."

"Oh yeah?" he said with a chuckle. "That's a good one."

"Yale not Brown."

"Ahh. Still. Christmas? For money?"

"Never pimped yourself out, Salem? Sold yourself? Your talents? Maybe for less than your worth? Maybe for more than you felt worth? Peut-etre... maybe I enjoy this."

"Okay. Fair enough. Christmas though? No family?"

"Maybe you're the Messiah?"

At that Salem laughed loud and hard and hit her with a pillow. "Now you've gone too far. Blasphemer! Witch!"

Danielle feigned outrage, grabbed another pillow and hit him back, laughing.

After a good round of pillow fighting, Salem's mood shifted. He plopped face down, pouted then spoke, his voice low and reflective. "You know, Danielle, I don't want anything. I wasn't gonna do this... I've never done this! But I... I didn't want to be alone tonight. Understand? I just want you to stay with me tonight, as long as you can. That's all."

Danielle's gaze softened. "Understood. It's a slow night. We're having a half off sale on would-be messiahs, half off the entire night. If you change your mind..."

Danielle undressed to her panties and slid into bed beside Salem, spooning him.

The room fell into quiet, their breaths the only sound.

An hour later, the light was out, and they lay together in embrace beneath the covers. Salem slept soundly in Danielle's arms, better than he'd slept in ages.

Early Christmas morning, Salem stood by the bed, fully dressed and ready. He watched Danielle sleep, a faint smile playing on his lips. Blowing her a kiss, he mouthed, *Thank you.*

From his bag on the dresser, he retrieved a yellowed newspaper clipping. Unfolding it, he read the headline:

A Grim Christmas for Killingworth as
Amtrak Claims Another Life.

Salem's expression hardened momentarily. Folding the article, he returned it to his bag and zipped it up. He stood there for a moment longer, staring at the bag. He left the bag where it was, emptied his wallet of all his cash onto the dresser including a $100 bill and several twenties and quietly exited the room.

Beside the bed, on the small table, he had left another gift. Atop a pile of his steno notebooks was a note:

Merry Christmas, Danielle. Thanks for the company. Here's a story to tell your grandchildren.

The taxi pulled up to the small motel. Salem climbed inside, shutting the door behind him. A few minutes later, the taxi drove off, leaving him alone in the morning sunlight.

He began walking across the snow-covered field, his breath visible in the cold air. Overhead, the countryside stretched out in a peaceful expanse, the snow lightly blanketing the ground. His footsteps left a clear trail as he moved steadily forward.

Eventually, Salem reached a small group of trees. He paused to get his bearings, then continued onward through the small woods that ran alongside a creek. Across the water, parallel to the flow, lay a set of railroad tracks.

His gaze fixed on the tracks. About a hundred yards downstream, a narrow wooden footbridge spanned the creek. He set out toward it.

As Salem walked, the words of a Tom Waits song played in his mind:

When you walk through the garden, you gotta watch your back. Well, I beg your pardon, walk the straight and narrow track. If you walk with Jesus, he's gonna save your soul. You gotta keep the Devil way down in the hole. He's got the fire and the fury at his command. Well, you don't have to worry if you hold on to Jesus' hand. We'll all be safe from Satan when the thunder rolls. We just gotta keep the Devil way down in the hole.

The crunch of snow under his feet was the only other sound as he crossed the bridge. Across the tracks, in the distance, a small, abandoned house stood in a field surrounded by woods. Salem began walking up the tracks in the direction he'd come, his eyes never leaving the house.

His thoughts turned inward.

Could that have been her house? he wondered. He didn't know. Ten years had passed. It occurred to him that he'd never bothered to learn anything about the woman killed by the train. He realized he didn't even know her name.

How many times had I read that article? Terrible. Merry Christmas, Mrs. So-and-So, anonymous dead citizen of Killingworth, Connecticut. God, what a waste of synapses I am. What an evolutionary joke.

Salem's internal monologue broke as he began speaking aloud, his voice rising in intensity and volume as he addressed the sky.

"Yes! That's right, God. We're better than you now! We've figured out ways to cheat death... okay, we're not quite that far yet. But boy jolly gee whiz, watch us prolong the inevitable ad infinitum! Yes, here we have several examples of human genetic misgivings who would never stand a chance in the wild but who are now living happy and productive synaptic lives inside the prison of their own heads thanks to our genius. Mr. and Mrs. Profoundly

Palsied will likely be rewriting the science books and making Star Trek fiction reality in no time thanks to the fact that they are not burdened by the distractions and sinful temptations of copulation and massive drug and alcohol consumption that led to the type of brain degradation and evolutionary treason exhibited in this sorry human specimen over here!"

He paused, pointed at himself, and whispered to the heavens, "That would be me, Mr. God, whose name I do not know."

Salem resumed walking, his tone quieter now but still laced with self-loathing.

"Yes, here we have a man, a shameful excuse for a man, who for reasons unknown to any of us, can't quite cut the sociological mustard and so seeks constantly to lose himself in alcohol and drugs and in so doing has so polluted, diluted, and convoluted his God-given brain that he can't remember jack-doodly-squat about what he did a week ago or ten years ago or who he was with yesterday or..."

His voice broke as he squatted on the tracks, his shoulders shaking with sobs. His tears dripped onto the cold steel, his cries echoing faintly in the stillness.

A voice interrupted.

"What are you doing?"

Startled, Salem stumbled sideways in the snow, his eyes snapping to the figure standing a few feet away on the tracks. The woman in the blue dress, smoking a cigarette, regarded him calmly.

"Why are you here?" she asked.

Salem scrambled backward, his voice trembling. "I came here to..."

"What? To what?" she pressed.

"To see this place. To try and understand."

Her laugh was instant, sharp and bitter. "Understand? Right. Jumping in front of a fucking train? That's understanding?"

"I don't know," he admitted, his voice breaking. "I'm lost. I'm tired. I drink too much. I pop pills. You did it."

The woman exhaled a perfect ring of smoke, her cigarette seemingly untouched by time.

"Look, being dead ain't fun. You think it's all bad, being drunk and crazy all the time, huh? Being dead, you don't get to get drunk. You don't have the option to get cancer from smoking or fry your brain with drugs. You don't get to choose. You don't get to make love here. You don't get to smell the downy heads of newborn babies. You don't get to howl into the wind and feel it in your hair. You don't get to do shit. All you get to do is watch. Big whoop."

Salem stared at her, speechless, as memories of his life began flooding back—moments of love, joy, and connection interwoven with pain and regret.

"Have you ever heard of the phenomenon of the Puer Aeternus?" the woman asked.

"The wha..?"

"Puer Aeternus. The child god. Eternal boy? Forever young? Dionysus, Narcissus, Icarus? No?"

Salem frantically shook his head, ever watchful to see the train come around the bend.

"Peter Pan?" the lady in blue said.

Salem nodded slightly, his expression revealing an awareness of

Peter Pan.

"Aha! Light dawns on Marblehead. Yes, Peter Pan. Carl Jung talked about the phenomenon of the grown-up who never grew up. The alcoholic, the addict, the trauma survivor. They are the lost boys and girls, everyone.

"What are you talking about?" Salem looked over his shoulder at the approaching train. It appeared to have stopped. No, he thought, not stopped but skipped, as if he were viewing a recording of a train on a scratchy DVD. One moment it rounded the bend and the next it shrank back, then came on again.

"I'm talking about YOU, Salem. You came here to see me. You were looking for an easy way out. Jump in front of the train, boom, splat, Salem flat, road pizza, done, baked, out of the oven in time for Christmas dinner. Very dramatic. I've got news for you kid. You are not unique. Get in line, take a number. Everybody wants to die."

"What?" Salem shook his head like he was evading a buzzing gnat.

"Self-destruction is humankind's first and greatest romance. Sound crazy?"

"Yes! Totally. Are you seeing this? What the fucks up with the train?" Salem gesticulated wildly in profound bewilderment.

"Don't worry about it. Look, think of me as your oracle, Salem. That's why you found your way here to me. Not to die but to be reborn…" The lady in blue went into a little trance dance swirling her lit cigarette around drawing a figure eight in the air. She sang the rest. ".. away from lands so battered and torn."

"That sounds familiar," Salem said, his attention still riveted to the train in the distance.

"Jimmy Hendrix.

"Where's the damn train? I heard it coming...

"HELLO? Are you hearing me? Yes I stopped the train. Well, not me but IT. It stopped it. Quantum physics shit. I said don't WORRY about it."

Suddenly Salem's legs gave out, and he squatted down on the tracks. He put his head in his hand. "I'm so confused."

"You know why they call alcohol spirits?" she asked. "Because it is a cheap substitute for REAL spirituality, for real transcendent experience. Bottled spirits! Djinns! Why do you think Muslims are scared of alcohol? Because they come from the deserts where every bottle had a genie in it. Alluring and catastrophic. Those three wishes never end well.

Salem, you, me, him her we all ceased to grow emotionally the moment we reached for that bottle or pipe or spoon. You stopped growing Salem. You are a mental midget now."

"That word is offensive to dwarfs, you know," Salem mumbled through his hands.

"Okay, you're a gnosisistic gnat. You have the emotional maturity of a midge, an annoying little black fly. Why? Because growth happens through hard choices. When you take that drink rather than think, rather than act, you stop valuable life lessons in their tracks."

"But the train? How the.."

"FORGET ABOUT THE TRAIN!" the ghostly woman shouted. "It's not your time, Salem! It's not your train. What the hell is the matter with you?"

"Auurgh. I feel like haunted winds are blowing through my hollow bones all the time. I mean, I am literally a train wreck. Depressed, anxious, panic attacks. Suicidal…"

"You don't want to die Salem. You want to live. Somehow your generation seems to have confused the two. Boredom I guess. I don't know. And it's gonna get worse in the next few decades. Terrible ennui. They ought to rename this country the Etas Ennui. That's French by the way. Etas Unis plus ennui."

Salem looked up from his hands and shook his head in annoyed wonder. "You are not at all what I expected."

"Yeah, well, maybe you watch too much TV."

"I don't watch ANY TV! I hate TV. I read books. Always have."

"Good for you. Technology of the future."

"You mean the past?"

"No, no I don't. Live well into the next century, and you'll understand."

The lady in blue dropped her cigarette and snuffed it out with her boot.

"All right my boy what's it gonna be? Life or death? End or new beginning? Think quick."

Just then Salem felt a vibration in his feet and heard the resumed rumble of the train. He noticed that a full lit cigarette was back in the lady's hand and that the train was coming again.

"You know what I'm gonna choose, don't you? Dammit what do I do?"

"Nope. Free will, kid. You decide. A future with pretty Miyanna, raise little Salem as your own. Or eternity with me right here by the tracks."

"Geez. When you put it like that."

"I put it like that."

"Thanks lady in blue. I'm sorry you had to die."

"Goodbye Salem."

The murmur of the freight train quickly grew into a roar.

Just then the squeal of the locomotive's breaks shattered the relative quiet of the forest, followed by the blare of the horn.

The lady in blue stood swirling her cigarette and chanting to herself. The orange glowing ember traced an infinity symbol in the cold air.

"Life? Death? Life? Death? Life? Death..."

A thought seemed to occur to the lady in blue, and she suddenly leapt through the air. In front of her, Salem still stood on the tracks, a glazed look of shock in his eyes. In the knick of time, she knocked him clear of the tracks. As the train screeched over and through her, she vanished in a puff of smoke.

A moment later, Salem found himself sitting in the snow. As he regained his senses, the train cars rolled by quickly at first and then slower and slower as the brakes caught. At last, the cars came to a shuddering and clanking halt.

In the sudden stillness, something caught Salem's eye. He swung his legs around and crawled not away from the train but toward it.

Smack in the middle of the coal car sufficiently distant from either set of wheels, there on a railroad tie burned a full lit cigarette. Quickly Salem scampered under the car, grabbed the cigarette and crawled back out.

"Jesus Kee-riced, boy!" shouted the engineer now standing over him. "You scared the living dolphin doo doo out of me. What the hell are you doing out here standing on the tracks, son?"

Salem lifted the cigarette to his lips and puffed. There was a long pause before he spoke.

"Healing," Salem replied in the high-pitched voice of one holding a lung full of smoke. With that he exhaled a giant plume of smoke and the exhaled breath of the living. The cloud of breath, hot just a moment ago, glowed blue in the frigid air and congealed like a genie forming. It appeared for a moment to be a woman in blue.

Later, wrapped in a wool blanket, Salem stepped off another train at a rural depot. He approached a payphone,   lifted the receiver, fished for a quarter, dialed a number, and waited.

"Hello? Miyanna, it's Salem. Is your invite still open?"

He smiled as the train disappeared into the forest behind him.

* * *

For sleeping people, those not truly living in the moment (and philosophers reckon most of us are these), death is scary. Others experience life's pain and pleasure with such intensity that LIFE is the scary thing. These most often turns to spirit and djinns. Death to them becomes an ally, a falsely alluring escape. Still others have it all figured out and live in a state of constant bliss. Me? I'm still mad as a hatter, but it's a good kind of madness, and I'm content to live it out. History is full of stories of sleeping people who wake up, and of lost souls who find their way before it's too late. This was my story, the story of Salem and the lady in blue, the train I took and the train I let pass by.

EPILOGUE

You will be happy to know that Miyanna is not the codependent enabler she appears to be. Immediately following a week of the sort of torrid love-making that comes of love-at-first-sight and inadvertently slathering Salem in overflow breast milk, Miyanna said "Salem, I love you and I see that you are telling me the truth when you say that you are not well. Let's get you some help." Utterly grateful to have been found by such an angel in his darkest hour, Salem voluntarily went right into detox in early January. Thanks to a trust fund apportioned her from the fortune amassed by her great-grandfather, inventor of the railroad knuckle coupler, Miyanna sponsored Salem's recovery.

Detox was followed by a three-month stint at Four Horses, a rehabilitation center in the Chiricahua Mountains in Arizona. In between visits to Arizona during his recovery, Miyanna did some nesting and found them a lovely home on the shores of Cape Cod, a place she had seen in a dream.

ABOUT THE AUTHOR

Rick Mc Kinney

Rick is grateful to still be alive after surviving migraines, anxiety, depression, PTSD, a trailer fire in Joshua Tree, drowning off the Lost Coast, and partying with Charlie Sheen. Rick passed through Checkpoint Charlie during the Cold War, had a beer with Chris McCandless, interviewed Julia Butterfly in her tree, drank wine on a train with Jac Holzman, dined with Kelly Preston and Mary Crosby, went thrifting with Robert Downey Jr., talked weltschmerz with Werner Herzog at a funeral, whitewater rafted the entire Grand Canyon, and walked the length of California and the entire Appalachian Trail (writing a book along the way). True to Gonzo form, Rick was uninvited from Hunter S. Thompson's funeral for drunk dialing Owl Farm the night before with an Aspen ski resort heiress. Rick is a writer and found-object artist and has made 10 art cars including Duke, a feature of Art Car World in Arizona. Rick has been sober and consequently far more productive since 2010. The author lives alone in the Arizona desert with his five ferrets.

BOOKS BY THIS AUTHOR

Mallmart Boy

The wolf child of retail

When a baby appears in a big box retail store in New Hampshire, it's up to ghosts Frank & Orlando, founders of Mallmart, to care for the infant & raise him the Mallmart way. Like Mowgli raised by wolves, Sam's childhood is unique. Hiding by day and roaming the aisles by night, Sam is king in a world of toys and goodies all for him. Sam develops a uniquely consumer-driven sense of the world and his own slang language of retail slogans. When love for Jackie sparks his discovery at age 17, he is just what a material-weary world needs to renew its faith in the shopaday life.

Dead Men Hike No Trails

An Appalachian Trail memoir written daily from the trail

"Following a friend's suicide in 2003, I faced my own suicidal depression and a choice. Dwell in grief or run gonzo crazy and free in the opposite direction, blazing bright and deep in the jungles of America, hiking and writing until my feet and fingers bled with a pure, honest, screeching love for life." Lending levity to tragedy, author Rick McKinney loads readers into his backpack for a 2000-mile Appalachian Trail odyssey, dealing a passionate, endorphin-fueled gonzo blow to suicidal thinking. Dead Men is a deeply empathic, unorthodox prescription for a nation depressed. It delivers an endorphin charged blow to a Prozac-dependent world.

Black Hole Son

One poet's quantum journey to save a lost generation

It's May of 1994. Kurt Cobain has tragically taken his life. Young poet Caesar falls through a time-space portal from a utopian reality into the summer of Gen X discontent. Kurt Cobain is dead and so are the hopes and dreams of Caesar's creative friends Tavi Xandman, Phat Jimmy, Lindy Lovecheeks and Phosphor Essence. Concussed from banging his head on entry, Caesar can't remember much and can't believe how bummed out everyone is. He must rely on his inner sense of self-worth to pull up the nose of their metaphorical Gen X jet before it crashes and burns. Black Hole Son is The Breakfast Club meets The Wizard of Oz. Written in 1997 and thrown in a shoe box, this book literally traveled through time and space to get here.

Made in the USA
Columbia, SC
17 April 2025